About the author

More poet than prose writer – the first book, *Waiting for Pat,* had to be written. The second, *Lyrical Mallards*, was written. It's solely down to Austin Macauley for the two books, and Arthur H. Stockwell Ltd, for the poetry, that my work saw some kind of light at the tunnel's ending.

Dedication

George, Adele, Harry, Daisy.
The Present.
The Future.

Peter Asher

LYRICAL MALLARDS

AUSTIN MACAULEY
PUBLISHERS LTD.

ISBN 978 1 78455 708 9 (Paperback)
ISBN 978 1 78455 710 2 (Hardback)

www.austinmacauley.com

First Published (2014)
Arthur H. Stockwell Ltd.
Torrs Park
Ilfracombe
Devon
EX34 8BA

Printed and bound in Great Britain

Acknowledgments

To Richard Stockwell. "Straight Arrow."
The man who targets truth every time. Of my poetry – his
"almost flawless" aimed me onwards, when I'd lost my faith in
any kind of target.
All my books are due to him. He alone aimed me out the
darkness.
Best buddy. Best advice.
I owe him everything.

When Not To Say Pardon

Lancival Ratatok was so named because his father wanted him Oaked 'Lance' and his mother wanted 'Percival.' 'Lancival' was a compromise agreed in haste as the Chief Oaker had to be elsewhere soon, and the squabbling parents were getting on his nerves.

The Family 'oaking' name, 'Ratatok,' dated back to the great ash tree which supports the world. The original Ratatosk (with an 's' lost over time) would run up and down the ash carrying post from one branch to another, and the present-day Ratatok family claimed to be descended from the divine Post Red, as they called him. However, Lancival, the subject of this story, was a doctor by profession.

On the 'oaking' evening of his Reddening, the baby squirrel who became a doctor had been given the traditional acorn to keep him quiet. While he was occupied, trying to nibble, ten Red Elders placed ceremonial oak leaves round the rapidly running-out-of-patience-with-his-nut youngster. The Chief Oaker bounded, his tail flourishing, deftly to the three corners of the triangle of ash branches placed upon the leaves with the most fidgety and by now angry youngster in the centre. The Chief Oaker had hurriedly recited the Oaking Vow and loudly blessed the name Lancival Ratatok, but the child ran out from the triangular circle in squirreline tears. While his mother stood looking on he begged her to show him how to access acorns. For squirrels, baptismal ceremonials are always frantic.

Dr Lancival Ratatok sat one morning drumming his fine long tail in thought on the leafy surgery floor. He was recalling what his parents had told him of his own 'oaking' and the Reddening, or dedication, of his name. What had brought this to mind, was the pregnancy of Geraldine Fitypatrick Nutter, grey squirreless of this parish. It had been a difficult 'confinement,' as Dr Ratatok preferred to call it and not the modern, post-antibarkterial term, 'furkin,' taught at medical school.

The word 'furkin' in squirreline usage served for both the act of begetting and the job of carrying the squirrel-to-be. (Indeed, 'fur' and 'kin' was a rather clever collocation and 'infurence').

Wood medicine in general had been transformed from simple potions of berry-boiling hopefulness to cure most things, more or less. The breakthrough was achieved by the invention of the antibarkteriotic, derived from growing cultures of ash-tree-dwelling insects and stamping on them. The pulp thereby obtained could be injected using pine needles. Different insect pulps were used for treating different diseases.

Dr Lancival Ratatok stopped tail-musing and sighed from beneath his snout-tipped glasses; it was the sign of the infinitely caring squirrel, which is a sign to behold in its pained squirrelfulness, unique to the species. Wearily he went to the oak shelf in the hollow oak where he held his daily surgery, morning and afternoon. The non-working days were Sundays, bark holiday Mondays (in honour of the Father of Barkteriological Medicine), annual Seagull Holidays (taken inland) and Annual Furry Holidays (taken on the coast). This seagull/mammal habitat exchange provided welcome breaks for many species unrelated other than by their thoughtfulness. The Ratatoks, like everybody else, enjoyed their breaks.

The elderly doctor was well ready for a break right then, in fact – Geraldine Nutter's confinement, as already mentioned, having been a particularly problematic one. Dr Ratatok's intuition – he did not profess to be an expert in squirreline gynaecology – was that Geraldine was about to have a difficult birth.

This was not unusual in squirrels giving birth for the first time. The thing was, she dreaded giving birth. She hated pain.

She was daily becoming more hysterical, refusing her nuts. She was so overwrought that her husband wanted her to have a caesarean — a procedure he'd read of in a rain-soaked magazine he'd found in the woods. However, no one else in the wood knew what a caesarean was.

Lancival Ratatok spent some minutes perusing the medical books as he'd done regularly ever since Geraldine told him the way she felt. What was wanted was a quick way of giving birth, but there wasn't one.

He was roused from the tomes by a yell of one of his twin sons at his surgery entrance. The Doctor went to the hole in the oak and looked out, still with his reading spectacles over his whiskers.

"Is anyone there, Lochran, other than us?"

"No, Father- unless it is the gentleness personified in this place of hallowed healing and nurture. For, as always when I deliver your postal keys, I feel the largesse of your goodness as an entity in itself."

Lancival Ratatok peered ruefully over the top of the wrong spectacles.

"How much?" he said.

"Four, Father," answered Lochran.

"When back?" asked his father.

"A week Friday, Dad."

The old squirrel nodded briefly. Then he went over to the medicine chest and took four sanctified ash keys out of a jam jar beside it (after first bumping into the chest and removing the wrong glasses so he could see what he was doing). While he did so, the Doctor's post-squirrel son (Ratatoks are usually postal workers, refuse collectors or doctors) placed the day's mail on the chestnut desk.

In this wild part of Lincolnshire (which wishes to keep its wildness anonymous) ash keys are of immense value to most species. Unsanctified, they are used for writing upon and mailing. Sanctified, they become money.

The exception to this is all the weasel family, including badgers, which for some inexplicable reason prefer aphids. Aphiols are hugely unstable as a currency, but ideal for posting as they find their own way there.

Lochran Greystone Ratatok was always broke, as teenage squirrels often are, so he often exercised his poetic talents on his father.

After the poet, Lochran, had thankfully left, and no one outside required a consultation other than on money, Dr Ratatok read his mail. Here was the key he'd been waiting for Dr Graham Hazel, renowned songbird, forensic and gynaecological thrush, had agreed to see Dr Ratatok that afternoon.

The key had come first class, which was a good sign for, in truth, Lancival Ratatok did not get on well with Dr Hazel. He thought him arrogant, opinionated and far too high chirpy of denomination.

Mrs Annodine Ratatok (Annie) insisted her husband had an overfull stomach before he left for Creature Comfort Cottage Hospital, where Dr Hazel held court. Dr Ratatok didn't like bounding about or conducting business on an unstable uncomfortable stomach, but he didn't dare offend Annie either. Gastric agony was the lesser of the two evils. By the time he was shown into Dr Hazel's office by his pretty female starling, elderly Dr Ratatok had been sick twice on the way there.

"Have a potion, old friend," giggled Graham Hazel musically, the 'old friend' delivered in an ironic squeak.

Nurse Starling eyed her superior sharply bringing him to immediate heel.

"Thank you," said Dr Ratatok, fearing the worst as Dr Hazel took his pipe out of his beak.

It is the filthy habit of many woodland creatures to smoke. Birds especially indulge in pipe after pipe of ground eggshells, which they maintain is good for keeping their lungs strong for whistling or taking deep breaths while flying.

"Reamer, Nurse."

Nurse Starling waited until Dr Hazel said 'please' and then, in her sassy female starling way, beaked him a beak full of scalpel. He proceeded painstakingly, by bill and crosswise-held scalpel, to scrape the bowl of his disgusting briar onto the desktop.

"This has to be prepared fresh, Lancival. It's my own unique answer to certain age-old medical problems. It had been lost for at least 5,000 years until I rediscovered it in bed the other night."

Dr Ratatok, though dying, was intrigued, especially by the bed, but he was too near death to pursue the subject. Apparently the old doctor had been asleep himself for the last three hours, sleeping off what was left of his dinner, in a heap on the floor with his dinner.

"You've been quite out of sorts for a while," added the young physician thrush, twittering merrily.

"We left you to 'sick it up,' as we say in modern medical parlance, while we prepared this burnt reed-warbler eggshell, parsley and wood-spurge inhalant and infusion. Go on – have a sniff."

He held the vile, stinking, black-contented lidless pot under Dr Ratatok's whiskers. As the old doctor had only just been awakened from a feverishly miserable sleep, and did feel pretty poorly still, his will to politely pardon himself both from a sniff of it and the involuntary breaking of wind after it was rather undermined; yet how much better he felt as he bounded home through the wood securely clutching his pot!

Dr Hazel's words clanged tunefully above his happy hangover.

"Knowing of your furkin young lady squirrel's difficulties from your ash missive, I wanted you to receive this potent preparation fresh. That's why I brought you here. It just happens to be good for bilious attacks and gastric disorders as well as maternally afflicted squirrels!" he added, as if pleasantly surprised.

15

"Why, Lancy Ratatok, you look quite the young brush. If that's what organic horse-fern faggots do for you, we'll have them for supper, too," exclaimed Annie with a wink which her husband thought quite unseemly.

"Your tail does take me back!"

Dr Ratatok, however, had no wish to be taken back.

"I haven't time to waste, my little fur cone," he said, taking care to emphasise 'cone' after 'fur' to avoid any tasteless confusion. "I must be away to give Mr Nutter this. It's for Geraldine's problem."

"Will it work?" Annie looked admiringly at her good and honourable husband, with just a tiny bit of regret that Dr Ratatok deliberately failed to notice in the corner of her eyes.

"It'll work, my love – and quickly, which is what we need," said Dr Ratatok, bundling his unusually lavish tail out through the cottage door. "Clean her passages, dearest, as it did mine."

Needless to say, it did. But – do you know? Geraldine Nutter also neglected to say pardon. With so many sets of paws to look after, maybe that was excusable.

The Squirrel and the Unicorn

Lancival Ratatok hated treating unicorns. The Doctor disliked it intensely because unicorns are so good at treating themselves. Overindulgence is their main problem, and when they're very fat they do need outside help. So good are they at treating themselves that, as likely as not, they're often unwilling to pay for treatment.

Self-pampering and selfishness have been the downfall of the whole unicorn race. Dr Ratatok in his time had tried to slim four entire unicorns – not, Odin forbid, all at once, for that would be impossible to get paid for, but separately over a long and infinitely wearisome career.

The first was a fat mare called Enid. Her stallion, Bartolini, brought her to see the young bushy, stethoscope and freshly qualified general-practitioner squirrel, and Dr Ratatok had never forgotten it. Eight years of strictly controlled fodder deprivation and counselling hadn't lost Enid an inch, but it had both greyed and fattened Bartolini immeasurably. As aforementioned, unicorns are naturally overindulgent and they go over the top totally when stressed. The by then less bushy stethoscope doctor had two massive unicorns to slim; and when the mare became pregnant – Odin knows how, for such huge beasts are unfit for procreation and parenthood – he had three; but unicorns are made for wishing on and with, and their desires (and ours) are best satisfied, being easiest, when most basic – or base.

A fourth unicorn came a little later, when the obese young stallion was followed by an obese young mare. Now there was an entire family of avoirdupois unicorns – but not all, thank Odin requiring treatment simultaneously. The parents died relatively young of obesity (Bartolini had been a heavy dung smoker as well). This left only the two youngsters, who, of course, took time to fatten beyond belief and become a real problem for Dr Ratatok.

The youngsters – being innately self-centred – didn't miss their parents.

The two gigantic burial mounds caused landslips in four cornfields surrounding the wood. The result, for the farmer, was a head-scratching loss of crops. Moles and badgers, and anything else that could shovel, beetle or beak, worked to repair the damage, -partly out of kindness, but mainly because they wanted to be rid of the unicorns, which were universally disliked because of their famine-inducing appetite. The enthusiastic digging led to a revenue increase for the heavily insured farmer, who never lost anything he couldn't find again and sell at a profit.

The two unicorn carcasses were effortfully disposed of little by little by perspiring ants, who cut them up, and rodents specialising in chemistry (as rodents do), who used plant substances to dissolve them. It was a long and smelly process and we needn't dwell on it – other than to mention that it forms part of the overall unpleasantness of Dr Ratatok's memory of caring for unicorns in the community. It was also why he was up at midnight, under the moody moon, lit by the eyes of nosy night creatures and the odd miner's-type fairy lamp.

For a restrained second time only, under the rainy cold-nose-droppy circumstances, he swore mildly in Nordic. Dr Ratatok spoke Viking fluidly when angry – as he mildly was right now – it being a fluid evening. It was of no use. The old pen torch he had found on the moors with two batteries in a lunch box lost by a workman working on the four fallen fields was lost again in the paw-sucking mud of the midnight wood when the Doctor stumbled and fell tail over tonsils. It was little consolation that Ransid, his other twin son wouldn't have to steal batteries from shops any more.

"Worry none, old chum."

The dulcet tones of Swami Krishna Mole met the squirrel's mud-waxed ears. "I heard you sploshing gently through the mire and fortunately you found me by habit, instinct and, mostly, my spiritual magnetism."

"Yes, of course," snapped the old red squirrel, more irritated than impressed, as he puffingly slid up and down the soggy slope.

On the top of the hill the Blessed Mole stood on his hill on his head in a rodentine yogic headstand.

"Why, Venerable One, can't you conjure up a ladder after all these years I've been struggling up to see you in all weathers?" Dr Ratatok more swam than asked.

"Material things are not for the enlightened," replied Swami snuffily from his Nirvanic molehill.

Dr Ratatok muttered bubbles in Viking, saying that ladders aren't material; they are ladders. Then he swore again in the tongue even sanctified moles aren't conversant with.

"Stop there, Lancy. I'll come down to your level."

This Swami did, deftly dropping from the headstand into the lotus rodent and sliding to base camp, to which Dr Ratatok had just beaten him another claw-clenching time. The two friends sat, lotus side by drenched-tail side, in silence but for the rain and the sniggerings of unseen night-timers.

"Have you seen anything of it, Lancy?" Swami spoke conspiratorially from the heart of his lotus.

The Doctor nodded and gave a slow, drippy-whiskered negative. "It's an ugly rumour – but ugly enough to ruminate over," Ratatok said.

"I agree." The lotus rocked from side to side and Swami continued profoundly, "The rumour is a tumour that can fester for us all if the tumour from the rumour has no root in truth at all."

Swami turned his wise but lotusly painful head towards the Doctor, who he thought would be impressed by his deep medical metaphor. Dr Ratatok turned in turn to meet Swami's sagacity-filled daylight-blind eyes with a lashing whiskery turn of unimpressed anger.

"Look, Krishna. Unicorns are trouble, and even the tumour of a rumour of one is a growth on every creature's happiness. They're greedy, wishful and lustful. We've enough of those already without them coming along as honoured high priests."

The lotus tightened at the thighs excruciatingly, outwisdomed and involuntarily awed.

"It's no time for navel-gazing cleverness – whatever navels are. It's time for getting to the truth," continued Ratatok awesomely.

Swami collected himself and thought a moment.

"Navels, I believe, Dr Ratatok, are either oranges or sea battles seagulls speak of that humans have from time to time to relieve their brazen boredom."

The squirrel eyed the mole archly, as if 'brazen' was a word maybe better not used by one who balanced on snout and sat cross-pawed in (obvious to a doctor) quite shameless discomfort.

From out of the black silence of the wood at 1 a.m. (that's 'silence' to the romantic and 'damn noise' to any animal trying to sleep) came giggling, swishing and the patented miner's type fairy lamp held by Feebie. She plonked lamp and bare midriff down beside Swami, whose lotus tightened even more, and she smiled her wickedly beatific fairy blue-irised smile at the two old rodents. Dr Ratatok's tail began to dry in the heavy rain at the sound of Feebie's voice, and her bare midriff gave the rumour of a tumour – a focal point for him and Swami to concentrate on while listening. (As fairies, by the way, don't have navels, puzzles can never be resolved by gazing at one's midriff).

"Your other son, Lochran, told me you'd be here tonight, Dr Ratatok – and I guessed what for."

The fairy voice was like that of the goddess of the wood, only with a stone-ground throat from smoking too much catnip To say she wore only what was necessary for a wood fairy is true – or perhaps she wore a little less than was necessary. The clothes on her legs, arms, back and neck wouldn't need changing, wet or dry – ever. The remainder wouldn't need drying much at all.

"There are no unicorns round for miles. Those two – Enid and her old man – cleared off years ago when you got that 'Unicorn Go Home' petition up and everyone signed it but us fairies. Living legends are good for the libido and fairies know it."

"Then what's been seen by at least a dozen worthy eyewitnesses – all independently and all (most of them anyway) respectable and upright citizens and insects of this wood?" asked Dr Ratatok earnestly.

"Come on, Ratatok," drawled slightly Feebie. "You've been around a bit. You know what's going on. I'll bet they come to you for pills to stop 'em doing it before their wives find out!"

Lancival Ratatok went red under his fur – for red squirrels under their fur have white skin, surprisingly.

"It's spring – as if I needed to tell old tight-up Lotus here beside me. He's been to you for pills as well – hasn't he? Special sanctified and venerated ones so he can say they're for his rosary if Millicent catches him."

Neither rodent replied.

"It's spring; horns of one sort or another are often seen in spring, whether they're there or not. Overexcitement and more wishful thinking with every May that passes! Snow's ended woods down to things so few and nests to do – and one's never too old to remember not to forget if a winter's moult can help it. Isn't that right, old fellows?"

Neither rodent replied.

Unicorn sightings did continue for a while, but not for long. The respected male wood dwellers – many in important positions on tree-creeping committees, etc. – spoke less often of unicorns as word spread that wives were in danger of hearing it. As Dr Ratatok made his way home in the watery light of a nose twitchingly beautiful sharp dawning of a fine day after a wet night, he thought that no matter how much he aged he never aged enough not to wonder. There's been a lot of prescriptions lately to write out for males of all kinds. Now he knew why – and why it hadn't happened to such an extent in other springs. He also knew why unicorn sightings hadn't been seasonal – until now.

He bounded up short, stopping yards from his dwelling. Annie would be making breakfast as she'd done since time immemorial when he'd been on night calls or business slogs to Swami's hill temple. Annie was lovingly, loyally, wifely – and old fashionably. Had his Annie ever gone about with a bare midriff? Would she ever? Of course not – unicorns or no unicorns – he hoped. Old-fashioned, that's what she was, and that's what he was. Yet the times in the wood they were changing. And maybe fat unicorns would soon be what everyone wanted to be; basics. Wishing for them, longing for them – instead of just letting them happen. That was base – dwelling on them; Dwelling. The word reminded him he was close to home and, shaking his head from side to side, he dashed, more than dragged himself, no matter how weary, towards the door.

Lyrical Mallards

Fame is always difficult to deal with, and more often than not will deal its recipient a blow sooner or later. To Lochran Ratatok, fame's blow came sooner, a little later, and much later still as well.

The first blow fame gave the handsome teenage red squirrel was having to give up his job as trainee post-squirrel on account of the lady squirrels swooning at their doors and chasing him on his rounds, squealing and carrying on, hysterical for the hairs of his tail as souvenirs to drool over by moonlit ash trees.

This was bad because many a good idea had come to Lochran Greystone Ratatok in the silence of those infamous mornings and also he genuinely had enjoyed meeting creatures on his rounds – so many characters to study and incidents of wood life to imbibe in friendly discourse with finch or ferret. Gone – all gone!

Why gone? Because quite literally Lochran Ratatok had awoken one morning to find himself famous in fern, fur and flower. The young poet achieved success overnight with the publication of his first slim volume of ash keys, entitled *Lyrical Mallards*.

The book was dedicated in honour of his favourite poets, William Wordsmouse and Samuel Taylor Coal Tit who's *Lyrical Salads* had been published 200 years earlier for a luncheon at Felixstoat to commemorate the fourteenth anniversary of Crown Prince Pheasant's giving up pecking at his food. *Lyrical Mallards* not only sent the girl ducks crazy, but it did the same for every female creature in that lost Lincolnshire wood.

"You've done it now, Lochran," said his father, Dr Lancival Ratatok (whom the hapless poet venerated), encouragingly that first morning when his surgery was under siege by unimaginable females of every species. "Just look out there, women for miles and your poor mother clinging to her nuts and mine in fear for her sanity. Is this what you call being famous? Is this the price of half a dozen half-baked poems about the egg-bound affair of Romeo Coot and Juliet Moorhen, with the daftest plot ever about a mallard revealing to them the unsuitability of their liaison? It thus turns out to be a tragic tale of unrequited love."

Lochran came out from beneath the table hurting himself as his tail snagged the strap of his mail sack.

"Father," he said, dull-eyed and tremulous-whiskered, "please ask my brother, Ransid, to do my round for me today. I dare not risk your having to face life without me."

Weeks had passed since then. Lochran had reluctantly resigned before he got his sack and he had taken to meditating at night with an autumnal dock-leaf cloak wrapped about himself and a deep-red petal cravat at his neck. As most nocturnal creatures aren't the least poetic it was cold, but at least it was safe.

From those tentative and innocent beginnings would over time develop perhaps the greatest satirical squirrel the wood has ever seen. From early tales of confused waterfowl and swashbuckling buntings would evolve, during a relatively short but immensely eventful lifetime, those biting satires and scourging commentaries on ladybird low life and leaf-mould goings-on every adolescent spider now studies in school or collegiate fen for reed warblers.

But this particular chronicle celebrates the humble beginnings of both a unique talent and a definitive personality that would change the literary underwear of the undergrowth forever and develop youthful innocence through tempestuous experience to less than youthful insouciance.

He would change form gifted but guileless to wood-worn genius in a series of horrifically difficult lessons, the first of which was bawled by life at the young poet about ten days after his overnight loss of the post job and concerned his new job's proclivity for bother with women – which, as all poets know, is a real bind.

The first woman to bother him directly, and not with him under a table and her outside, was one who subsequently turned out to be his tutor, friend and confidante, and thus his worst bother of all.

"For a start there's the dreadful subject matter of those related odes in your rotten *Lyrical Mallards*. I mean, a couple of unrelated ducks having an unrequited nesting site. It's loopy, naff, boorishly inane and claw-cringingly embarrassing; a coot and a moorhen, moonstruck, gazing into each other's bills until a wise old roué of a mallard comes along and straightens 'em out. I sent my mother a copy in Australia and she flew back here in disgust to personally fling it at me!"

Lochran thought to question Feebie on this latter point, knowing fairies cannot as a rule fly such distances, but he daren't. He remained silent as Lady Feebie Melbourne (the family name originated when her ancestors were banished from the wood, for misuse of spells, to the world's only fairy penal colony, in Australia) continued her tirade against the young bard's muse.

"My poor ancestors went to Australia in wing-shackles and made good through the sweat of those very same wings and the continued misuse of their spells. That's how they became rich and titled – through sheer effort and spells of service to the ruling kangaroos and dodos of the time. Who do you think got shot of the dodos? We did, when it became obvious, powerful as they were, that they hadn't got two brain cells between the whole lot of them to rub together – for setting fire to their backsides in order to get the idle buggers off the ground! Survival of the sharpest it is – nature's law – and to hell with the fittest! The humans always get everything wrong."

"But, Feebie dearest, how does this fascinating information concern me? I made my precarious way through undergrowth the log way around, avoiding all females including a human teenager walking her bitch – just in case both of them had heard of me – because I desired your estimable advice on how to be more worldly of bearing, less shy and more assertive of eye, tail and deportment ."

"Shut it, Scribbler, and listen!" Feebie interrupted angrily.

"Stop drivelling like a runt-of-the-litter gnat begging a flea not to bully it, and speak like a red-blooded red squirrel! Even your dad, old as he is, doctor that he is, doesn't whimper round the long way with his tail in his teeth. Not him! He's a real squirrel! He's got that certain smoulder in his eyes that smokes women out and that deep but gentle squeak that'll ground any fair fairy and send lady squirrels into tail-thumping raptures. Dr Lancival Ratatok's got it, and all you've got is ruddy ducks who don't know their heads from their harbours and end up lovelorn and suicidally polluted by self-administered overdoses of oily water bill full, dying in one another's wings down by the crisp-factory outlet pipe! A multi-species of barmy female come flocking after you – that not so much minor as minuscule poet whose ash keys penned such tripe, and that same tasteless little worm of a squirrel. And you do nothing more about it than hide, tremble and carry on as though you are William Wordsmouse himself, flitting through the corn with four tiny mincing paws and a constant wary eye in the air for a poetry-hating goshawk! I'm a bloody lady, Lochran, of fine birth and penal heritage, but even I don't talk like a mouse's muse and I never cower before (or after) butterfly, beast or human!"

At that moment, Ransid Ratatok was heard coming down the mud furrow outside Feebie's consulting nook with his bag and beech spike. He was calling out Lochran's name – brazenly brave – with a few assorted females in tow.

Ransid, a refuse-collecting squirrel by vocation, was enjoying fame vicariously as Lochran's twin brother, a good half-second older than his brother. Ransid was a typical, cheerful teenage squirrel, into typical, teenage, cheerful squirrelesses, acorn balls and folk songs.

After jovially scuttling to and fro, packing in and off three giggling stoatesses and arranging to meet one petite grey squirrel under the fallen oak for some flirting, he bounded up to the window. Carefully he looked about over his shoulder and, gauging that the clearing was clear of females, he stuck his pointed stick through the fern lace curtains and into Lochran's ear.

Lochran yelped like a stuck squirrel and both Feebie and Ransid shushed him.

As the ear only bled a bit, Feebie got her ash-key diary out and made an appointment for Lochran to see her at the same time the next morning before Lochran got change to – or even thought about, or even intended, dared or wanted to – ask for further sessions like that day's.

"You'll have to watch her, Greybrick," (This was Ransid's pet name for his brother).

The teenagers were grubbily making their way home through the grubs in the undergrowth, desirous of not drawing attention to the famous young poet.

"Mum told you all about cross-species flirting, same as she did me, and Feebie's a soddess for it."

Cross-species flirting is practised universally in the wood. It is a quite innocent outlet for animal hormones of every shape, age and size. Nothing ever comes of it but a little playful feather, fur, mandible or antenna touching at its very worst; ever since some of the more ugly outcomes were banned by folk law long ago.

Ransid stopped crawling, spat a grub out and raised his head through the teasels.

"Come up, laureate – it's as safe as crow's milk," he said.

They were close to the filial ash and continued the remaining distance upright.

"Why does she want you to go back again – or what's her excuse, rather?"

It was Lochran's turn to stop. He turned to answer his older brother, "Because she likes my eyes, she says they're like Father's only weaker of hue and content, but they have the modicum of a spark of potential."

"You mean she thinks *Lyrical Mallards* is lousy and she wants to personally help you write the next wood bestseller by furthering your broader education along certain lines – right?" said Ransid.

"Right," said Lochran.

"She also wants you to stop speaking like a lovelorn coot and talk and act like a younger version of your dad – am I not right?"

"Yes – you are not incorrect," Lochran replied, downcast and doleful like a downcast and doleful doe. He widely stared into his brother's woodly wicked and wood-fulsome eyes. "How did you know, Ransid?" he queried timorously.

"Because, me being older 'n' wiser then you, Dad told me how her mother did exactly the same for him when he was a shy young intern squirrel fresh on the female wards."

Lochran pondered a moment before enquiring, "But I thought the Dowager Lady Berenice Melbourne lived in Australia?"

He had a dreadful premonition, which surprised him by its rather woodly waggish anticipation of Ransid's answer when it came a moment later. Indeed he turned out to be correct, but it gave him no pleasure. Ransid informed him that she'd lived in Australia ever since 'The Scandal,' as he put it. Lochran did not desire to know more. He did, however, always look back on that as being the moment a satiric squirrel of a poet was initiated.

It was also the time when he began looking on his dear father as just maybe – like all the very best saints – something of quite a reasonable sinner as well. And, as with all baptised poets – as with all true ostriches – just maybe was quite enough for Lochran Greystone Ratatok's rabid imagination to dig its head in the muck whenever it found it from then onwards. So doing, he was able to see far further than most.

Life's Little Anvils

Dr Graham Hazel was not used to fear. It did not sit easily on his beak. Young, handsome, in the full feather of his thrushhood, Graham Hazel should not have been – as he was that gloriously mocking morning – frankly, scared wingless.

Mocking mornings are those when you feel glum but the sky is laughing, showing its blue teeth and pointing at you, derisively wagging its white fluffy clouds breezily. It's on days like this that your anvil breaks. But if you were Dr Graham Hazel, forensic and gynaecological thrush, your anvil would have broken the day before at breakfast, while Nurse Starling was laying out your snails as you like them. Promptly he'd ordered another, more utilitarian, model with an additional groove on the edge for smaller shells and a collection of moss fitted underneath to keep one's tree base tidy. Nothing is more off-putting to important clients with chrysalis or duck dignitaries than an untidy tree base. Dr Graham Hazel was most fastidious in the conducting of his practice – as much so as he was in his gorgeous appearance. But that gleefully cruel morning the renowned thrush's spots were somehow more matt, as if he'd forgotten to preen. His eyes were not their usual birdly confident almost kestrel-hawk piercing, but furtive and uncertain like little wrens in a garden full of big lads, reticently looking about. Nurse Starling reluctantly had to admit to herself that her boss and chief flirty were egg-bindingly scared.

Suddenly there came a wing on the visitor's branch. She looked up. From the size of the feet it was Chief Constable Coal Tit. In a nutshell, he'd been expected.

Superstition is a superstitious thing. Thrushes as a species are not infamous for it, as are creatures like humans and woodlice. Graham Hazel was the exception. Most thrushes accept the breaking of an anvil as a big part of life. If smashed one meal, you get another – end of it. But to Dr Hazel it was an ill omen of more bad luck to come – and, to be fair, it did come, that very same evening. Only hours after the anvil's breaking over breakfast he had seen a death's-head moth. Indeed one had almost settled on him up his tree. Death's-head moths are not ill omens to anybody as a rule, but in Dr Hazel's already heightened state of nervous twitterbility this one was.

Chief Constable Coal Tit was a personal friend of the young doctor, and he had helped solve many a crime for Forest Forensic Division over the seasons. When the bat had arrived with the midnight ash-key mail (unsanctified ash keys are used for writing on in the woods) he had read the message and returned his own via recorded-delivery aphid for additional speed, to the effect that he'd flutter round sometime the next morning – which he had. Hence his huge police tit's feet (in comparison to his body) were now on the visitor's branch. As Nurse Starling had sent all that day's scheduled clients home with the excuse that Dr Hazel was shell-shocked, there were no interruptions as Graham Hazel, too shrilly for auditory comfort, reflected his fears.

"So it just broke, Graham – just like that, eh?"

"Clean in two – as if tampered with," came the chilled reply.

"But haven't you had anvils break before? I mean, everything breaks – hearts, legs, anvils ... Nothing lasts forever but crime, I always tweet," said the philosophical tit.

"Yes, of course (I hope) – but never followed by a death's head moth. That's a threat, planned and engineered by my enemies."

"And who might they be, Graham?"

"That's for you to find out, Chief. I'm a doctor, not a beak – in that sense, as it were."

Chief Constable Coal Tit, being a thoughtful sort of tit, sat on the branch, surveying the woods. His wings were folded behind him in the time-honoured all-species-of-constable fashion. His friend Graham had obviously been working too hard for too long. What he needed was less work and more worms for a while. Maybe he also needed an intimate holiday with Nurse Starling; maybe not. That would be both offensive and an offence, technically tweeting, against nature, though the joys to be got out had to be weighed against the risks involved. Repercussions might involve an egg of indeterminate colour and the ensuing horrible beginning of DNA egging paternity chirrups.

Such idle – and rather unseemly – musings were brought to an abrupt end by the topmost branch's noting of a movement below. It turned out to be Dr Lancival Ratatok, no doubt on his daily nest-and-burrow calls after surgery. Chief Constable Coal Tit swooped impressively fern-wards in his white-and-black uniform and perched on a low-bushed hawthorn just in front of the elderly red squirrel.

"Good day, Coal, my old friend – how goes the policing?" asked Dr Lancival Ratatok, out of breath.

"I'm worried about Graham."

"Me, too," replied the squirrel a little too quickly and emphatically for comfort when hawthorn spikes are up your bottom and even the smallest shock can be injurious.

"He's cracking up, isn't he, Lancival?"

"His anvil too, so I've heard, Coal," came the reply a little too painfully quick again.

The Chief Constable felt it prudent to get off the hawthorn and head for the clearing ahead, where he and the squirrel might converse less spikily.

"It's his own fault, though," offered Dr Ratatok.

"Working too hard?" offered Chief Constable Coal Tit.

"Not a bit of it!" replied Dr Ratatok, offended.

"Whatever do you mean?" snapped Chief Constable Coal Tit offended in turn.

"Hazel's young, thrushful and strong as a weightlifting heifer, only he's – too imaginative, let us say," opined the old GP, coming to a halt near an old pine. "All his lot's hedgy. They never stay perched for long. Really the species is too sensitive and fanciful for its own good," he added, shaking his head, which was red with the white streaking of greying age.

The Chief Constable couldn't help commenting, in spite of the seriousness of the situation, that his old friend was going grey rapidly, to which the squirrel replied that, even as a grey squirrel, his wife Annie would still recognise him though some of his red-squirrel patients might leave the practice.

"Then what's wrong with Graham, Lancival?" asked Chief Constable Coal Tit after a moment's self-absorption, absorbing the profundity and sarcasm of the red doctor's last words.

"He's ready for a weekend away with Nurse Starling, that's what," said Dr Ratatok. "Badgers what's done and not done." Then came an expletive. "Too much nerves and not enough nesting's no good for any bird. Oh, I'm not condoning anything incorrect for a moment – it's just common sense. Nurse Starling looks pretty and can talk medicine all weekend. Dr Hazel talks like a nervous wreck and can look at Nurse Starling all weekend. It will do them both the woods of good."

Chief Constable Coal Tit thought silently about this. "But what if you're wrong and some enemy or other really has got it in for Hazel?" he said at last. "What if you're wrong Lancival Ratatok?"

The only one who's got it in for him is Stoned Weasel. He'd do anything for an impressionable species as long as it paid well in sanctified keys. Thrushes are brave, but their artistic streak leads them into dodgy dealings. At once they're both sensitive and forensically sound, but they're stupid also and easily led by their aesthetic misjudgements. The idiot ordered an ornamental anvil, carved at one end like a female thrush's tail with its feathers spread. Pornographic, it was – and a good thing it is that it was of cheap sandstone and

33

couldn't take the force of having snails percussioned on it week in week out.

"I see," chirruped Chief Constable Coal Tit firmly. "But what about the death's-head moth? How do you read that, coming so soon after the anvil-breaking?"

"That was Marlene – none other than her, poor dear."

"Not."

"Yes – the young widow whose Frank was so cruelly taken from her by that human moth collector."

Chief Constable Coal Tit wondered only briefly what a collector of heinous moths would make such a fundamental mistake as to bag a death's-head one. The Chief Constable could be slow sometimes.

"Oh, I see – a heinous collector! Right, right, but what was Marlene doing round at Hazel's?"

"I sent her with Walter's new catalogue." Dr Ratatok was firm and precise, straight and to the point as always.

Chief Constable Coal Tit absorbed the import of the statement. Then the reed dropped like a penny.

"Oh, Lancival Ratatok, you cunning old squirrel!"

"That's right, Chief Constable. Poor Marlene makes wings meet by taking out the weekly free Ash Key Times giveaways – various leaflets, keys and key catalogues. Legitimate firms, like Walter Stoat Mason Ltd, give her commission on any custom she finds for them. Marlene's mother-in-law happens still to be out early in the morning owing to her getting on a bit and rather losing her sense of time. Things were different when her hues were the shade of youth and her death's head had more teeth. She was overhead just as Graham's beak cleaved the anvil in two. Terrible, she said it was. That such a brave thrush, with such a reputation for daring and alacrity, should have overworked himself solving crimes to such an extent that his feathers now quiver at the rending of a brick!" Dr Ratatok fell silent. As he finished, his ageing snout pointed paw-wards, obviously moved.

Had the Chief Constable not being inwardly smarting, he'd have seen a snout tear glisten down red fur.

"Graham Hazel, for all his derring-do and skill, doesn't solve crimes, Dr Ratatok; he helps our constabulary tits solve them."

Lancival Ratatok's head rose at the note of offended twitter in his friend's hurt squawk.

"Oh no, my dear Chief – I didn't mean he solves things without you. Not a bit of it!" corrected the squirrel apologetically. "Look – by the time Marlene's mother-in-law had got to me on this and I'd sent my lad to Walter's for a catalogue and my wife, Annie, to fetch Marlene, the day was tired enough to call it a day. Graham was frightened by Marlene, taking him a catalogue – too late, as it happened, because he'd already bought a more bog-standard replacement anvil off Stone Weasel again. Some thrushes never learn! It might be, though, that Graham wants to keep in with Stone because of his undergrowth connections – who knows? Anyway, it meant Marlene was too late to get any commission. You can chirrup in if you like and give a key or two. Coal – as I did when Marlene came back with nothing but a split lip from Graham Hazel's frenzied wing tip flailing in fright." All at once Dr Ratatok fixed his eyes on the Chief Constable, concern in his caring dark old eyes. "I think we ought to fly and bounce over to Hazel's place and see how he is," the squirrel concluded.

When they arrived, a message mat of keys was placed upon the thrush's tree to the effect that he'd been called away on urgent shell shock, but would be available on Monday morning as usual.

"Best thing for him!" puffed Dr Ratatok. "Too much forensics makes Hazel a dull thrush." The squirrel turned to his feathered friend of many a long winter's moult.

The Chief Constable said simply, "I hope he's careful, that's all." To this he added, "He's had enough of life's anvils of late, without little feathered ones around his neck with their worms up his beak."

Al Cacone

If Dr Lancival Ratatok ouched at all, he ouched deep inside as now a Ratatok finger screamed quietly to itself and its owner. Long ago a bouncing baby red squirrel had learnt how stiff upper whiskers were best for parting leaves and fixing situations.

The handsomely ageing squirrel stepped back a paw or two and frowned at the bill he'd just hammered with trusty ashen mallet to the tree. All morning he and his wife, Annie, had been busy bashing bills to trees the wood over while a locum, young Dr Juniper Adder, newly graduated from Medical Barn, conducted his practice for him. The bill poster read:

'To whom it may concern –

Concerned families and loved ones: Do Not Do It.'

'It' was nuts. Ratatok had a pretty good idea his son Ransid, the dustman teenager, was doing nuts. Why else would he lose bins so often? Why else fall over regularly? Apart from that, Lochran, the other son and poet, had told his dad that Ransid did nuts.

Nuts were a huge problem among teenagers. It was the culture – the thing to do and chew for the young of most species ever since the sixties, when the woods went free and barmy morally squeaking and parental discipline took a duck-dive.

While musing and looking upon the bill, Dr Ratatok became aware of Grisum Tuft's long, hairy arm, slightly slow and perfectly obvious, making its way around the trunk and across the bill from behind the tree. It was obviously Tuft's arm because of the bandage over the infected tattoo Dr Ratatok had bound at surgery on the previous day. Not only that, but another giveaway was the scarring from all the other tattoos that had likewise gone wrong, requiring medical attention.

"That such a hairy ape should have such a bald arm!" pondered Dr Ratatok.

Before the red squirrel had a chance to squeak angrily, "Get your vile paw off, Chico!" Chico had gone off at speed, clutching the ripped-off poster in his vile paw.

"Why do they call Grisum 'Chico,' my dearest?"

Dr Ratatok hadn't noticed Annie arrive beside him. Before he'd a chance to answer there came the distinctive and unmistakable sound of fern and branch and hare meeting awkwardly some distance ahead.

"The hare has come to grief, Annie," observed Dr Ratatok solemnly. "Let us find out why he's taken the bill in such a rough and roguish manner."

Annie adjusted her new fur-do and followed her husband into the darkly green moss before them. Not far had they ventured when Chico was found wrapped around a branch by his long ears with his huge-footed form dangling. All about him were scattered bills, presumably ripped from each tree the Ratatok's had put them on. No sooner had the sorry-looking hare not answered the Ratatok's enquiries than the ferns parted and two evil-looking grey squirrels appeared.

The one-eyed one spoke first, the patch bobbing up and down blackly as the long, wicked nose twitched: "Don't you meddle in fings what don't concern you, Dr Ratatok. Mr Al here's got the woods sussed. You leave us alone and we won't bovver you one acorn's worth of peewit eggs."

"Why do they call you 'Harpo,' Clarence?" asked Dr Ratatok, in no mood to be intimidated.

"On account of his mother's proficiency on the instrument," replied Mr Alphonso Cacone, nut baron and general do-anything-there-is-to-be-done, no-good, nefarious trafficker of pine-tree produce within the woods. However, this said, apart from being a gangster he was a surprisingly honest estate agent and conveyance for all creatures wanting woodland property. That alone was why Dr Ratatok tolerated Al and medically attended to him and his gang members – a motley collection of hares, who all like helping to cause trouble, and grey squirrels, who know nothing else but how to cause it.

Dr Ratatok was in no mood to fence around with words or dally with his son's sanity – such as it was.

"Look, Al – you get these woods clean, you hear me!" Dr Ratatok's squeak could come across with a rich and commanding timbre when necessary. "Get your foul nuts away from the teenagers of these woods and make your fortune selling homes in holes to tree creepers. Don't do nuts on the side or you're a dead squirrel, you hear me!"

By now Dr Ratatok's squeak was really scary – enough to make Harpo retreat a bound or two. Al, however, stood his ferns.

"I see," he giggled in that infuriating way grey squirrels have "And you, my good doctor, are going to dead me, are you?"

Grey squirrels aren't good on grammar, especially when excited or emotionally involved. Dr Ratatok knew that a bit of wordy whisker-teasing wouldn't come amiss.

"Deader dead you'll be than the dread discomfurture you harbour would be if treated by an expert in the field of the dread-making – dead-making – disorder of whiskers – blighting nit disease." Then, after a pause for the paw he'd placed in a fist beneath his snout to theatrically come away, Dr Ratatok delivered the coup de grace to the by now rather uncomfortable-looking nut baron.

"That very same fatal disease you presently have a-twitching and a-spreading about your afflicted personage and poorly, poorly whiskers as I glare at you this actual woodedly frozen moment in time."

Both grey squirrels' jaws dropped to order, for grey squirrels – even gangster ones – are cowards when it comes to vague pains, dental fillings, piles or WBND.

There then came from above this tense grouping of desperate duellists an uncouth cursing, and Dr Ratatok recognised the voice of his son Ransid intermingled with the crisping of oak leaves being squirrel-handled roughly and the alarmed cry of an overpowered grey squirrel.

No sooner could 'punk' be said, than Ransid landed on the ground, but not before Silvan landed there with Ransid on top of him. Lots of leaves landed on all of them.

"Why do they call you Zeppo, Silvan?" said Ransid sarcastically, stuffing his snout into the wide, frightened eyes of the hapless grey squirrel beneath him. "Up a tree to no good, spying Zeppo was, Dad. What do you want me to do with 'im?"

Though Dr Ratatok was surprised to have Ransid drop in like this, he didn't wish to show it and spoil the effect.

"Let him up and shove him roughly beside the others, son," said the Doctor, getting rather carried away with the whole gangster thing.

"For Dillinger's sake!" exclaimed Al. "What do you intend doing about my WBND?"

"And ours!" snivelled Harpo and Chico.

"And his!" snarled Ransid, pointing a nod at Zeppo.

Lochran came forth out of the ferns, driving Al Cacone's BMW.

"Here 'tis, Father. I got some on my cravat and it's kind of rotted it, I'm afraid – but it seems to be the right potency because it stains so well."

"Smells so well, too," observed Dr Ratatok with satisfaction.

They scraped the brown preparation off the rear seat of the BMW and applied it by means of paw, feet, fur, snout and Ransid's head butts to the face, eyes, whiskers and all-over Zeppo, Harpo, Al and Groucho – or, rather, Al's ancient father, Ian Cacone (for some reason known as Groucho), who had ambled in on the scene inadvertently and didn't want to be left out.

When he'd finished smearing the preparations prepared by Princess, the sheepdog friend of the Ratatoks, and her bowels about the personage of the gangsters grey, Dr Ratatok stepped away together with his sons and scrutinised his cure at work stench and play.

"Now, foolish woodland gangland boss that you are, go home but don't wash for the next three seasons. Just roll in the back of the BMW. Should you disobey, I shall not let you have any more brown organic amelioration paste at the end of the lot you got piled on the BMW."

"And many thanks for allowing me to use that splendid BMW," added Lochran after his father finished. "It was such a thrill to drive the latest brown-mouse wagon – and a two harness job at that! Luckily Ransid and I watched you park before you came for your consultation with Father and we just knew you'd be all for us fetching your prescription medicine to save you time before feeling its benefits."

After the grey squirrels had driven off stinking, with Grisum Tuft, alias Chico, bounding slouchily behind, stinking even worse, Dr Ratatok, Annie and the twins sauntered and hopped bemusingly home singing traditional Nordic squirrel songs Ransid was telling his father of his investigation while Lochran led Annie in a particularly lovely rendition of a Lincolnshire folk song taught to Lochran by a drunken swan on the bank of the river near a pub in Brigg.

"So you see, Dad" shouted Ransid above the noise, "I got worried about my mates falling out of trees and waving their paws threateningly at motor cars. Pine nuts are lethal. I got hold of some and found out it's not the nuts that are hallucinogenic; it's the snail's slime Cacone spikes them with.

Suck a common snail and you get high – honest – and that's all there is to it. For all that Cacone and his lot are real barons, they might just as well form – oh, I don't know – a comedy act or something." There came a crafty glint in Ransid's eyes." All my mates now get high for free if they want by snorting snails. But you and I know snail slime is disgusting and no red squirrel worth his nuts if going to go near it, 'specially now the woods are waking up to Lochran's poem about the turn-on on pine nuts being snail slime! Me 'n'' Lochran spent hours going round sticking it to those trees Chico kindly made room for us on."

Before Dr Ratatok had a chance for this to sink in, Ransid suddenly ran ahead of him and in front of Lochran and Annie, still blithely singing away. Ransid lifted Lochran off the ground by his besmirch cravat with one paw. He glared up at the poet lofted high but not so mighty on the brawny arm of his punk dustman brother.

"I've been meaning to catch up with you," said Ransid, rather cleverly in view of the run he'd made in order to dangle his brother in the air. His squeak darkened and he didn't sound humorous anymore. "Clumsy I may be: stupid I am not. Why did you tell Dad I do nuts, Lochran? I'm good at climbing one-handed and here's just the tree for posting poets on – or from."

Furball Farm

The Wood Cup for football was held every ten years as it took some of the slower species of players, like snails, or those with little legs, like ants, about that long to get home from their final matches, have a wash and a bite to eat, do a spot of training and then get back in time for the start of the next Wood Cup tournament.

Lochran Ratatok hated all physical games and was only taking part because his self-appointed manager and mentor, his twin brother, Ransid, had threatened to head butt him if he didn't volunteer. Seeing as none wanted to open, close or have anything to do with it apart from players and fans, Lochran had no problems being accepted by FIFA, the Ferally Initiated Football Authority.

"They would do well," said Ransid, "to make full use of Lochran's girl-attracting potential. The young poet should attend as many games as possible."

Girls don't like football, but they did like Lochran. In fact, suggested a scheming feral friend of Ransid's on the board of directors, if it went unpublicised as to which games Lochran would be at, but publicised that each day he'd be at one or other of them, you'd have full female attendance everywhere! This was agreed unanimously by the entire board, comprising Ransid's friends.

By rights she oughtn't to have been the one doing it, but Shrewd Matthews was a soft old vole of an editor and, seeing how sad she looked, he'd told her to get out and on with it. Working on the bottom rung of the ladder as a junior reporter meant the best stories were covered by bigger rodents – bigger in the sense of more senior or better known. The Wooden Ladder, as the national daily to the local wooded areas was known, was called upon to interview the famous and eminently multi-species-desirable young poet Lochran Greystone Ratatok. He it was who'd be inaugurating the inaugural game in the Wood Cup between two opposing snail elevens – as Ransid had exclusively tipped off the newspaper.

As Elizabeth Tailor Shrew made her way through the woods, her tiny nose was damp with anticipation. This worried her because damp snouts are not considered decent among young ladies. Unable to curb its obvious enthusiasm, all Elizabeth could do was occasionally bury her snout in the grass or screw it into the ground. This made matters worse as the earth stuck to the damp and made it look as if she was wearing a muzzle – as if maybe she couldn't trust herself in the divine bardic presence.

Her anxieties only made the offending item wetter. She kept crossing her eyes to look at it, so Elizabeth kept bumping into things. One of these things was a squirrel in a red cravat. She immediately recognised him as Lochran Greystone Ratatok. He was carrying a football – or, rather, the Ferally Initiated Football Authority-recognised farm-cat manufactured fur ball for games between opposing mollusc teams.

"You have a damp nose and possibly a heavy cold, young lady. Make an appointment to see my father," advised Lochran, drying the damp patch at the shrew end of his trouser leg vigorously with the fur ball.

Elizabeth had heard of the poet's fastidiousness of dress and precise habits and her tiny heart both stopped and fluttered – alternatively, without endangering life, because now it had too much to live for. She regretted the unpromising beginning to their relationship, but was thrilled by the thought of any kind of relationship with this handsome creature, drying her end of his trousers at this very moment's rub in time. Lochran continued rubbing.

Elizabeth decided she must be brave and squeak up, "If you take off your trousers, Mr Lochran, sir, I can roll on them.

That would be better, for my body warmth will dry them more efficiently than that disintegrating fur ball."

It was apparent from the growing soreness of Lochran's knuckles that this was the case; Elizabeth, being one who squeaked quickly and repented squeaking at leisure, didn't realise what she'd said until she'd said it.

Lochran ceased knuckle-scrubbing on his trousers and, still bent forward and double, fixed her with the handsome eyes in the handsome raised head. His neck was at a most uncomfortable-looking angle, bent upwards from near his feet to greet Elizabeth. She tried, more unsuccessfully each time she tried it, to keep upright on her hind legs to make herself look more impressive.

"I admire your eloquence. It is unusual in the woods these days," drawled Lochran imposingly in a sombre squeak. "But I abhor your suggestion, which if taken at face value beside the wet-nose manifestations, would lead anyone of a less broad-minded disposition than I to be a trifle suspicious of your motives."

As if the sun had suddenly ordered fried eggs all round for breakfast on a dark day whose grey clouds expected to be in for dour meagre bowls of rainwater, the bardic expression lost all its stern squirreline angles. He grinned the red grin of a tickled-pink squirrel poetic genius.

"But I like you, young lady shrew. You're fresh, erudite and rather attractive, and you may accompany me to a football match!"

Lochran took Elizabeth's shoulder bag containing her ash key pads, and before she'd time to reply he was off up the path among the trees. Deep within the woods it is hard for humans to see the berry-dyed leaves of football-club colours flying on the branches of the trees. They were put there by Ransid and his board of enthusiastically devious rodents.

The poet slowed when he realised Elizabeth couldn't keep up with him, and matter-of-factly he asked her the question she was dreading, "What brings you this near a football match? I didn't think girls were into the Wood Cup."

There was no point in dodging about, shrew-like, and she couldn't lie to her hero anyway.

"Oh, Mr L ..."

"Lochran, my dear, dry your nose on my trouser hem," interrupted the poet.

"I'm a reporter for the Wood Ladder and ..."

"I know you are. I saw you at their offices in the holes under the bridge yesterday when I arrived too late to stop Ransid telling your editor I was to open, close and attend throughout the Wood Cup. Ransid loves the limelight even more than limes. He never considers my feelings," signed Lochran. Then he added conspiratorially, "Nor, my dear, does anyone else! I'm famous, but don't desire to be. I detest the world and its ways. Indeed, to be candid, I have never loved the woods either – nor the woods me – until recently. Only now do they love me because I'm something new for a weasel or two."

"But your great works, Mr Lochran – the beautiful 'Childe Sparrow's Orphanage?"

"Flippancy!" squealed Lochran in anguish. "A mere trifle, young lady. It was concocted merely to amuse. It's about a cuckooed-out sparrow youngster who opens a homeless baby-bird sanctuary for sterile starlings to come and foster out fledglings. It's a thing for the heart when I wish to – to change heads."

A little way ahead they could hear the slow munching of crowds of snail supporters waiting for a football match.

"I wish to awaken the woods to the miseries, indigestion and yet unalloyed loveliness of creaturemanity, and let them know football's a waste of clearings and of time."

"Then why not rebel against Ransid and those who wish you to be what they want?" ventured Elizabeth, becoming even braver, as shrews will.

Lochran stopped instantly – it was so unexpected that Elizabeth carried on and came back to him.

"Rebel!"

Lochran looked at her. He was a aghast as a gassed squirrel!

"I couldn't do that, don't you see? I must suffer Ransid's physical and emotional brutalities upon my person – and the slings and arrowroots the woods and world belabours me with; and why? Because poets must court suffering as no other creature in and out of the universes of men, beasts, bats, fairies and fireflies, etc., would deign so to do. The nature of the muse is mist," he added, head low and mysteriously, romantically, eyes opaque and filled with some kind of distant distance.

Little Elizabeth went weak at the knees and so flopped upon her tummy indecorously.

"Come on, my child – you must report for your paper and give the fern-bound masses that which their tiny celebrity-filled beaks and mundane-minded burrows of narrowness deserve."

Such a sign of aching suffering came from the great squirrel's being that Elizabeth closed her eyes, unable to stare, starry-whiskered, into his divine face any longer.

"Come," Lochran said, mood-changingly briskly. "Dry your nose on my trousers. We'll be late for kick-off!"

With that he bounded ahead of the young reporter, leaving her wide-eyed, snout-drooling and belly-flopped, to pick herself up and charge in a decorous lady-shrew fashion after him. Elizabeth huffingly puffed onwards until she saw Lochran stop again some distance ahead at a place where the sky alone faced him with its blue arms folded comfortably as if to say, "There you are, young poet fellow – there's your devoted audience waiting in the clearing below."

Elizabeth drew up beside Lochran. There, with a red squirrel plainly sitting in a glum pose paws to jaw and elbows knee-propped, was an empty clearing passing for a pitch. Hordes of slow-munching female snails, slow-milling like a slow-motion football crowd, were slowly masticating crisps on all four sides.

"That is my brother and twin, so they tell me, though I personally doubt the 'twin' and the 'brother,'" observed Lochran sourly. "Dry your nose on my trouser hem, young lady," he added absently.

One snail who'd been raisin her head for the last hour caught sight of Lochran and began a sort of drone or wail, which was taken up by every lady snail in the crowd of lady snails. Ransid stood as if bitten on his bottom by an adder with its tail in one of those sockets humans have in walls to make their lights work. His ears he pulled down the side of his head like an old fashioned bonnet, and before he was driven by the din to tie them under his chin Lochran dashed down the snail-free trail along which the players were supposed to enter the clearing. Lochran grabbed his brother's leg as he tripped, that being the nearest part of his body and both brothers sprawled.

"That's the nearest thing to a foul we're going to see in this Wood Cup," moaned Ransid as Lochran picked him up.

They made their exit back to where Elizabeth waited.

The cacophony the teenage snails made – and some old enough to be Lochran's grandmothers – grew in volume and intensity as the threesome retreated into the woods. It would continue for days as, once started, snails don't know when or how or why to stop. They are that slow. If a couple of newly wedded snails decide to part on their wedding day, they will be together for at least their golden anniversary. Understandably, Lochran asked Ransid what was going on, once they were far enough away to ask for, hear or make excuses.

"I won't lie, Lochran," said Ransid unexpectedly. It's all gone wrong. I've watched humans play football for years from the edges of parks where I hid. I thought it would be a great way to spend the winters in the woods too, but no one wants to play. At every ground on the opening day of this Wood Cup all that have turned up are girls of every fur, shape and wingspan. They've come to see you, Lochran!"

"But why didn't you find out if the males of the species want to play football and take part in the Wood Cup?"

"I asked some of them and they were all for it, but the fixtures clash with the humans' football season. The birds have gone to watch human matches from the steel grandstands, and everybody else wants to be in the parks or watching televisions from window ledges. Nobody's interested in the Wood Cup except the women, because of you!" Deeper moaned Ransid, and moanier still. "We don't hold the Wood Cup in summer because in summer nearly everybody wants to watch men play cricket."

So that was it! Ransid's idea of the board's selling Wood Cup memorabilia made of acorns and decorated with fur balls (by cutting the farm cat in on the deal) came to nothing. So did his idea for a special winner's trophy, a wooden spoon pinched from the farm kitchen and officially chewed by the board.

Instead, upon that day in every clearing in the wood, women and girls of all species wailed, cheered and crooned for Lochran Greystone Ratatok. Elizabeth Tailor Shrew went back to her newspaper with the story of how 'Lochranmania' was sweeping the ferns and fens and not football.

Ransid had the bright idea of organising an annual Lochran Day, so the females could cheer and shout in their own species' spectacular way. Naturally it would need a board and little beaver-carved models of the poet. Lochran said no and quietly squeaked to himself how grateful he was to little Elizabeth Tailor for pointing out that it was possible to rebel and say no.

Ransid, of course was infuriated. He was about to beat Lochran up, but Lochran got hold of the wooden spoon over in the corner and chased Ransid all the way to Fur ball Farm, where the cat and spoon lived.

Christmas Eve

Annie Ratatok brushed her husband's tail lovingly with a rat-jaw comb, as the Doctor brushed his teeth with a catkin.

"For the Sweet Squirrel of Odin's sake do be careful, beloved," implored she, opening the door for him to fall out of the tree nest, drop ten flights of branches and become fully awake by missing altogether the moss, fern and toadstools, and hitting instead the largest, most knobbly above-ground root their bad-season pine-tree home had to offer.

For this was the annual 'Season of the Bad,' that ugly period between Guy Stork's Night and Christmas Eve.

"Did you not see me signal, Father, as you fell through the air? A little left with your tail, I kept waving. If you'd done as I said, you'd have safely landed over here among the soft flora."

"Bugger bloody flora!" snarled Dr Ratatok at his poet son as Lochran's fine bardic features peeped from between the fully moonlit ferns – a little to the left of the painful right where the Doctor was examining himself for any sign of life. "How many times have I told your mother about that ridiculously placed ex-magpie nest she insists on us spending the bad season in? Conductive to night calls it's not Too high up and not safe. Damn thieving magpie! He blinks his black, shiny eyes, tells her it's well placed for easy access – which it is if you don't mind making exits on your arse – and cheap to rent at a mere 49.99 ash key for the period we need to be near Moss Side, where the silly celebrations are and all the mousine injuries happen."

Lochran made his way to his father's side and helped him put his spectacles back together.

"I've enough tapeworm wound round the broken frame already to do a whole wood's worth of birthday presents, thanks to Annie's allowing me quick access to oblivion on all six nights so far this bad season!"

Lochran, calm as unusual, merely raised eye brows squirrels don't have to raise but would often if they did. "Come, Father – it's not so bad. As always I'm here to greet you, help mend you and defend you as we make your mouse calls together – for I would not allow you to venture further into the Moss Side mousing estate alone."

As father and son journeyed through the moonlit woods towards the mouse number the Nightjar Emergency Flight had flown home to Dr Ratatok, Lochran enquired as to the nature of tonight's call-out.

"Nest 13 – Saffron Twitchtail's disgusting old reprobate father."

"What – Angus again?" Lochran was surprised. A mere few nights into the bad season and the fifteenth call-out in all, and this was the tenth to Angus.

"If only he'd leave off the farmhouse, stay out of its corners and away from the fuzzy crumbs and furry bits of cheese! He knows house fluff's a narcotic. If snorted, it causes anal fissures in rodents and temper tantrums in their children. In homes as badly heated as those in Moss Side there may be no escape from poverty and hardships – but hard cheese, I'm afraid. Fluff – or 'crack,' as we call it because that's where it's found (between floorboards) – is no way out."

"No, Father. In a mouse as ancient as Angus, all it does is irreparably stain his fur ..."

"And it makes him call us out every night at 3 a.m. to attend to his bleeding haemorrhoids," Dr Ratatok summed up for his son.

The Moon helped itself to see even more clearly by hitching itself up to a tall pine top. It was at that moment behind that same pine trunk, directly in front of them. Suddenly something was seen to move, by both red squirrels, who stopped, not so much scared as terrified. The bad season deep in wooded Lincolnshire is full of rumour and hearsay – and here, say, might be right now some ghastly legend taking form.

And so it was. Out stepped a heron, long-legged and dressed in a cloak of chicken feathers with a cockerel's tail stuck up from a bandana of dried chicken wattles worn around its forehead and sewn together with finest shredded ivy stems.

Pigs can see the wind – but that's just the beginning of it, for all creatures, excluding man, can see ghosts. This was the ghost of an obviously well-to-do heron with its proudly held beak and the usual ghostly aura which not only gives ghosts away but also indicates their social standing by its colour. This heron's was blue indeed – the blue aura of blue blood and long legs. However, the real giveaway as to this bird's true identity was the hen feathers. Only one heron in the whole of recorded history has dressed (for spite) in hen feathers – Guy Storks, aka Guy Heron.

"You're a doctor, aren't you?" enquired Guy's ghost.

"Indeed I am, sir," confirmed Dr Ratatok, trying to keep his quaking stethoscope still.

A silence followed and awkward, uneasy fidgeting ensued.

"Em, I need a good doctor. You are, presumably, accompanied by your son, who looks to me like a poet. I invariably trust poets, but I never trust doctors unless they are accompanied by poets. One doesn't find many poets wanting to be associated with doctors, so I presume this one must be your son. He looks fairly grown and could have bolted long before now. Though not conclusive, this leads me to assume you must be a fairly good doctor and reasonable father. Centuries I've waited for this, and now I see your stethoscope quaking. The impressive figure towering above you is all that enhances your diminutive self."

This speech complete, Dr Ratatok did not find himself immediately drawn towards its maker.

"You are Guy Storks, aka Guy Heron, are you not?" he asked, forcing as much disdain as possible from a too high squeak, his quaking medical instrument clattering against his belt buckle.

"And you are?" asked Guy Storks, upper beak superciliously crossing the lower slightly, with aristocratic disdain a mere doctor could never match. The heron's growing confidence burst like a balloon on his beak point. "You with the pink cravat go and look out for mice and warn me if you see any will you?"

Lochran, a little hurt at the scornful command from one who professed to be a poet lover, went off mouse-watching as told.

"Can you give anything to rid me of the pestilence of Moss Side, Dr Ratatok? I'm doomed to haunt it, and, as all know I'm abroad haunting on Guy Stork's Night, the mice, who dislike me intently, and all I stand for, come deriding me with cruel taunts, hurtful jibes and lousy poetry."

Lochran caught this and came a little nearer. Despite himself, Dr Ratatok was intrigued. He was also irritated, owing to the late hour and his awaiting mouse call being delayed. The Doctor was always diligent – even with ridiculously dressed herons.

"Was it not you who long ago, disguised as a visiting stork dignitary from overseas, came to disrupt the inaugural sitting of the Parliament of Fowls?"

"Yes, Dr Ratatok. I was planning to pluck out while they slept the feathers of ducks, chickens, goldfinches and wrens – those short-legged species who take it upon their brazen beaks to run the woods as they see fit. Small legs and big egos! Imagine! Wagtails – run a puddle they may, but never a whole wood! I wished to pluck eagles and I wished to pluck ducks – not as a foul act, but as a dire warning of the shape of ticks to come if I return and get really mad. Then a hen – a cheap, asleep hen – awoke as I pulled, and she raised merry hell. The parliament awoke, turned upon me, plucked me dry and hung me turkey-wise till dead. Yet I was as justified then as now in my public-spirited actions, for see about you how the short ones mismanage the woods and countryside. See how the miserable mice deride me; And why? Because I have legs to lead, they have usurped my rightful wing to power!"

"Ahem. Indeed, indeed." Dr Ratatok uncomfortably squirreled a throat clearer. "What do you want from me?"

"I want ..." began the heron before becoming so distraught that he had to break off and start again. "I want to no more hear hordes of stoned mice each bad season, chanting:

"Guy Heron, Guy Heron, you're a rotten, lousy plucker –

Tried to pull their feathers, but got thwarted by a clucker."

A lone beak drop dewed from his beak with the emotion of it all. The heron composed himself.

"You are a learned rodent – a scholar, regardless of small legs. Doctors, who know poets, have contacts. Doctors, who know poets, must be able to get me through to Christmas Eve."

As it happened, both Dr Ratatok and Lochran did know how to get through to Christmas Eve, they also guessed why the heron was so desirous of getting there. It was not too far a journey.

The voice of Lancival Ratatok, so darkly subtle and soothingly strong, called; then Christmas Eve came.

"Dr Ratatok! Good to see and hear you, Lancy! How may I serve?"

Dr Ratatok blushed, his natural rust turned fire-engine red. The divine presence sat on her haunches outside the sacred burrow.

"Eve, my dear," said Dr Ratatok, "Can you grant release from this mortal wooded coil and absolution from his chicken-feathered purgatory for the ghost of Guy Heron here (aka Storks)? He's had it up to here with mice and short-legged creatures in general and wants to be set free from earthly bondage and go to heron heaven to meet his Maker."

Eve pondered. "Devout, is he, Lancy?" she asked.

"I doubt it," Lancy answered.

Eve's beautiful, if divinely vacant eyes, shone so the moon could peek at them from another treetop it had found upon following the three to Eve's abode. Eve's nose twitched meditatively.

"It is my sworn undertaking to feed the starving poor upon my personal day, once each year. You who are better off are aware of how this is done."

Dr Ratatok and Lochran were well aware, but they were also well aware they would have to endure one of Eve's interminable lectures on the subject – the reason they went to see her so infrequently.

"All winter I stay indoors during the day and only come out to eat tree bark at night – unlike less divine rabbits, who eat indoors during the day, but come out at night to eat as well." Christmas Eve was looking directly at the Heron, who, judging by his gormless appearance, regardless of long legs, had no idea what she was hinting at. "During the day, mortal rabbits sustain themselves upon their own initiatives, shall we say. I do not. I save my own initiatives, day in and day out. It is upon my own initiatives that I feed the poor on my annual feast day."

"The humans always get it wrong, don't they, Father?" Lochran was about to become irritating in that know-all poet way which so got up his father's whiskers. They were relieved to be making their way back to landlord Magpie's dray. Lochran continued merrily upon his discourse as Dr Ratatok's mood of relief evaporated, "It was the human poet William Chaucer who wrote of the difference between how eagles and ducks make love, in his long poem 'The Parliament of Fowls,' you know, Father. It's so like men to misunderstand and get the wrong end of the bush altogether."

"Nothing to do with smooching, then, son, eh?" said Dr Ratatok interrupting in an attempt to stifle Lochran's interminable babble. "All to do with politics, actually, son isn't it? Humans think about nothing but muck, so their Parliament of Fowls has to be about ducks having it off. Typical!"

"You can be so crude at times, Father," observed Lochran.

"Only out of desperation to shut you up; sensitive souls, such as yourself, son, won't venture where uncouthness dares to hope."

They reached the trunk of home and Lochran was about to heft his father's backside on to the first rung of the ten flights of branches to Annie.

"Before I go to my bachelor poet pad, Dad, hidden from the various women of the wood's species, may I enquire about a point or two?"

Dr Ratatok sighed. "Be quick – I want to rest before daybreak, when Angus starts straining at toilet again. Thankfully he'll be out of it right now whether we've been or he's been or not tonight."

"You know after Guy Heron was persuaded to swallow the, er, silver-bullet pudding – the divinely treated initiative for releasing ghosts from earthly bondage – as prepared by her worshipful Eveship – and you and I, Father, had finished holding him down while she held his beak open and then tickled him under it to get him to gulp it whole, what did you mean? I mean when you said "Give over, Guy – stop complaining! Anyone would think you'd the holly as well to pass, as Eve's passed the pudding!" What did you mean Father?"

Expressionless, Dr Ratatok fixed with piercing eyes his poetic offspring. "Humans copy us – right?"

"Right!"

"You've looked through farmhouse windows and seen the large, round, brown plum pudding with the sprig on it on the day of the Lord Jesus. What does the plum pud remind you of? Something that's a miniature version of it? Is it not like a much bigger version of ...?"

"Oh yes, Father!" The ash key – if not the penny – as they say in the woods had dropped with Lochran.

"Then it only figures," continued Dr Ratatok, "That long years ago, Christmas Eve was none too careful when feeding the poor on her initiatives. Who knows what her initiatives picked up by way of bits of flora off the ground before she got better at it! There's many a sharp evergreen hereabouts after all. So there may have been many a nibblesome Angus, suffering posterior problems, way back passage-wards, in those days, don't you think, Lochran?"

"Yes, Father!" Lochran beamed his handsome squirreline smile. "Good thing humans have sense to leave the holly behind on the table," he giggled squirreled.

Dr Ratatok, who had just reached the first branch home, thanks to Lochran's shouldering him up, turned and sternly whisker-flicked his son in the eye.

"Good thing, you say, Lochran? Oh, such a good thing, is it, now?"

Lochran was saved from his father's fury by a high voice from high above them, "I that you, beloved? That nice nightjar's been back once more to day Angus wants you ever so badly. I just caught you in time before, poor thing, you're snug and warm in bed and have to get up and make you way downstairs again!"

A Master of Legend and Law

Father said it was a cuckoo. Mother doubted as it wasn't old enough to have gone off and got the red dye they put on sheep – if that's what it was – all over its chest.

"Yes, it was sheep dye and, yes, it is old enough," said Father in his dogmatic robin way. "If it is old enough to kick chicks out of nests – which it is – then it was!" he sputtered, beak-spitting all over his wife.

A robin's life is happy as long as it's not sad, and Mr and Mrs Tech Robin-Crimsonlake were not happy on account of a cuckoo/robin lookalike (maybe) masquerading as a child of theirs, but killing the other kids by chick-evicting. Murder by nest-eviction is a punishable offence in Lincolnshire woodland. It is cruel and messy.

The Robin-Crimsonlakes were a well-to-do couple with a plush bush and tidily kept dropping-area beneath their nest, but they had a dwindling crop of kids to show off this year. This situation had to be feather found around soon.

Mr Robin-Crimsonlake devised an infallible cuckoo-sorter-from-the-rest-of-the-boys test, as he called it. As it was spring it rained incessantly day and night, so the weedy-looking now sole inhabitant of the nest was told to sit still whilst the nest filled with water up to just below his meek little beak on this particular grey morning. Come midday, Mr Robin-Crimsonlake was in disgrace and Mrs Robin-Crimsonlake had made an appointment to see Dr Lancival Ratatok later that same day.

Colds, more colds, a verruca-pawed badger and an elderly vole's demise – that had been Dr Ratatok's day by teatime. Now this!

"This is not a cuckoo, but a shiveringly sick young robin, Elspeth. Antibarkteriotics I shall not prescribe for the gasping as we're in danger of overprescribing and weakening all species' immune systems." Dr Ratatok pulled thoughtfully on his squirreline goatee. A hint of eyebrow rose seriously as he authoritatively squeaked. "Pride yourself on doing all a good mother could by smothering baby George in body warmth, and elicit Tetch to jump about creating dry feathersome heat non-stop and wafting it George-wards."

Dr Ratatok removed the straw thermometer from the youngster's wing. (The thermometer was a clever device whereby if beak, floppy ear, mouth, wing or backside squashed the tube it would prove that the patient could exert pressure, therefore had a temperature, was thus alive, and could be treated).

"I suggest Tetch should stay awake, doing the same therapy all night. By morning all shivering – bar his own – should be gone. Judging by the pine cones, it'll be dry tomorrow," observed Dr Ratatok while studying the bent thermometer.

"But what about the mood swings, Dr Ratatok? Why is George a possible angel one minute, doing the nest for me on nest-room day, and the next murdering brutally the rest of my children?"

"Your distress I've noted – and with good cause, Mrs Robin-Crimsonlake. In birds the mood matters are more a flycological problem than a medical one. In this case, I think, shall we say, there's a dichotomy between good and evil rather apparent in George's behaviour. A visit to Swami might be initially prudent."

"Why ever the holy mole?" asked Elspeth.

"Because a young robin coming on demoniacally, deeply tweeting, frothing at the bill and shoulder-winging his siblings to their deaths – and the next moment doing housework and begging his mother to let him pop to the seed shop for a treat for his father's supper – hints at a spiritual anomaly."

Because Swami Krishna Mole sat on Holy Hill from dawn till elevenses and was open to all comers, regardless of species, incisors or seed, it was unnecessary to make an appointment.

"I thought," said Dr Ratatok, "that I should brief you on this puzzling case before wing." (The wood creatures always use the phrase 'before wing' because, if you look, there are no hands.)

Swami eyed his handsome old friend, bad-sightedly and ruefully.

"It's a spiritual one all right," said Swami in the sort of tones humans, especially are mechanics, adopt with customers. "I think I'll levitate, while I regress George under hypnosis. I'll get a good look at him from above see if I can feel the vibes and read any of them that are apparent."

The next morning was wetter than ever. Tetch flapped weakly, exhausted and sodden at the foot of Holy Hill while Dr Ratatok took his temperature. Mrs Robin-Crimsonlake and George were on top of Holy Hill as Swami put an extra thorn through his loincloth in preparation for not losing it during levitation – a phenomenon often experienced by airborne moles.

George, still shivering, was not made to relax by Swami, even after many attempts, just as his mother was not made to relax. She fluttered about disconsolately – and irritatingly to the holy mole. However, George was fortuitously induced to regress into a past life, to 'see where the sheep dye fits into things,' as Swami put it. When George became unconscious (the cold, damp, fever and shivering eventually regressing him to a blackout), Swami, clutching his sodden loincloth, attempted levitation thrice and each time rolled down Holy Hill, narrowly missing Dr Ratatok, who was busy administering antibarkteriotics to Tetch. The doctor was forcing heart-stimulating herbs inside Tetch's agony-clenched beak after the squirrel-tail thumps-to-heart resuscitation (a technique patented by Dr Ratatok's grandmother) had been applied when the thermometer failed to squash when placed between Tetch's legs and up his bottom.

Appearances are not always as they seem, though. Swami declared at the foot of the third slither down that the regression had been a complete success and that this unusual but effective form of levitation had enabled him to gather the information desired from George's subconscious.

An exceedingly grateful – tearful indeed – Mrs Robin-Crimsonlake and George carried Tetch homewards (his heart was now creaking but working, again thanks to the squirrel tail and the nearest wood-floor chemist), Swami having assured Elspeth that all was going to be well if they followed certain instructions he had given.

Squirrels hate mysteries nearly as much as going underground, so soggy and bedraggled Dr Ratatok listened while Swami poked his head up out of his molehill.

"It's an odd course of action you've adumbrated to the Robin-Crimsonlakes, Swami. Did you fiddle it, or is it legit?"

"You can be very crude and to the point at times, Doctor" came the reply. "But I'll tell you it's as legit and kosher as turning your back on a patient while beating seven air-bells out of him with a great red bushy tail, flailing him to death everywhere from beak tip to tail tip. Talk about cure or kill! Your grandma, Ratatok, must have been as hit 'n' miss at medicine as the humans' National Health Service, and I'm pleased I'm not being treated by either!"

Dr Ratatok, flooded, bedraggled and hurtfully deflated, was silent before simply saying, "And you can injure a fellow to the quill or follicle at times with that mealy mole mouth, Swami."

As neither wanted to fall out after their nervy and trying experience, both held their tempers.

Dr Ratatok returned to his professional enquiries: "Tell me, then, Swami, how you arrived at your conclusion."

"There's an ancient legend humans but not robins have," began Swami. "Robins get on with people -"

"God help them!" Both Ratatok and Swami said these three words together as if the synchronicity were preordained.

"Humans of long ago were not as beastly as those of today, so they needed a spiritual kind of reason to explain why robins have red chests. The folk who liked God claimed it was a robin that administered to and tended Christ's wounds on the way to Calvary. The red breast, they say, is the blood of Christ. On the other hand, folks who like the devil claimed it was a robin that took water down to hell and got singed red by flames while administering to the thirsty inmates."

"I see," said Dr Ratatok. It was raining at its springtime hardest and he wanted to get home, but he was eager to learn the truth – or the untruth, as it may be. "So on one wing you've the good-natured robin helping Christ, and on the other you've the one who's bad, but brave enough to help the devil keep his suffering souls happy by bringing drinks in on a regular basis. Great!" Dr Ratatok paused, turned, wrung out his tail and continued, "But what's the link between the legend and young George's behaviour?"

"There isn't any," replied Swami.

His spectacles, having previously been saved, buckled beneath Dr Ratatok's paws as the wire rims made their way slowly in the floods off Swami's nose and began to float down the hillside just as the Doctor's paws returned forward-facing after relieving his tail of unwanted gallons.

Having replaced the crazy bent frames, Swami continued, "I was fed up with the case, it being far too wet to levitate. No spiritual technique works well in a flood."

Dr Ratatok looked down upon the short-sighted mole, whose nose didn't even know his glasses were twisted. "It did for Noah. We wouldn't be here if his spiritual technique hadn't worked in the water."

"Yes, but he had a ship, didn't he? snapped Swami.

"Oh, and I suppose if you'd had one as well, you'd have levitated OK!"

Swami ignored the sarcasm.

"It's a good thing you're a master of legend and lore is it not, Swami?" observed Dr Ratatok dryly in the wet.

"It's a good thing the Robin-Crimsonlakes believed me when I said it was a sure-fire cure to get George into an apprenticeship as soon as possible and that his trouble was that he was bored with housework and killing and that the devil makes work for idle bundles of feathers."

There was an amiable quality to Swami's tone in spite of all the unwonted cynicism towards him.

Even Dr Ratatok was impressed.

"Quick thinking that!" Admiration was in the squirrel's waterlogged squeak. "Using both legends I suppose in some way suggested a cure for George's extremes of conduct – without letting him or his parents in on the legends."

"Yep – rather smart, wasn't it?" replied a bronchial Swami with pride. "Trainer bouncer to a tit club or goldcrest nightspot where the gay, bright and smaller-than-robins-but-rather-feral-tongued songbirds and high-flyers go by night and a student-ship towards qualifying as a male nurse by day! What about that, then?" his pride was by now bubbling nearly as much as the torrent.

"Fantastic!" So adamant came Dr Ratatok's adulatory exclamation that Swami was not expecting what came after the short silence, "Tits can be nasty and a bit of brawny robin is just the thing in its place to keep order. But what if the brawn gets out of place and order and starts evicting poorly little prematurely born infant dormice? How are you gonna keep the toughy tonight and the tender today? You can't control a legend with a job. And what if it all goes wrong and George can't hang onto a job? What will you do, Swami, when George comes back to you for further guidance?"

Swami pondered this. Any spiritual counsellor worth his salt water always sees further than most and meets possible problems with plausible answers.

"There's always the flycologist," said he in a way that hinted not of one who's put off or discomfited, but of one who's practical.

And Dr Ratatok said in a way that hinted not of one put off so much as of one who's both helpful and practical, "But before the flycologist why not get George, if he can't hold the jobs down, to show you how to levitate, lift off the ground – up, up and away, like the jobs?"

Tails of Justice

The earwig on the table behind him went off. Dr Lancival Ratatok stopped pondering at the surgery door, went inside, picked it up, clipped it to his long pointy ear and returned to the door. He faced the fringe of bushes on the other side of the clearing which patients would cross to come and keep appointments.

"Oedipus Rex, Ratatok. Can I come yet? It's wet in here and there are nasty, creepy things."

Ratatok raised a paw to shade his eyes and peered over towards the bushes to see if he could see his old friend. The hands-free (or, rather, paws-free) earwig allowed the Doctor to take calls while doing something else with his arms. (You can get run over by a fox if you aren't looking what you are doing when nutting).

"Not yet, Oedipus, Annie's gone to the bank. I'm waiting for her call; then I'll give you a buzz and you can come."

Miserable mutterings came from the other end of the line, and then a click as Oedipus disengaged his earwig from his ear by opening its nippers with the paws he'd been using to part the bushes so that he could see Ratatok framed in the doorway.

No sooner had Ratatok unnipped his mobile than it went off again.

"Oh, Lancy, there's such a run on the bank and all our ash tree savings have gone – stolen by desperate animals trying to retrieve their ash cash before it dies on them. What are we to do, beloved?"

"Go to your friend Jasmine Grey Tail and have a nut and a wink with her. A nice hazel kernel and a few minutes' restorative kip at a time like this'll set you up to see things in a different plight – if not light, dearest. I mean it's not that bad. We've been through worse. Remember when those bugs were spending it on food and eating the money – and then there was that run on the paper when rats tried to introduce thrown out old fish, chips and peas to the wood? They'd drag it from bins in town round the back of cafes, and after a few weeks when it was the in thing. It all fell through because you can't successfully carry a tatty haddock home in a handful of ash key wrappings. Remember those cold greasy chips we were slipping and tripping on from one end of the wood to the other, Annie? Dangerous as hell is was."

(Note: as you probably know from your reading books on Lincolnshire woods, only young, tender ash keys are used as currency there. Old, tough ones make good general-purpose paper – though not for greasy chips as seagulls would have caught on if they were.)

Annie squeaked a weak "Yes, love" and agreed to go to Jasmine. "I'll feel more myself then," she said.

"Sorry, angel, I'll have to go – patient at the door."

Ratatok unnipped his phone and bounced to the door, surprised by the loud urgency of the knock.

"I will not spend another ruddy minute in that wet clump, Ratatok, for you or any squirrel else!" exclaimed the bedraggledly seething Oedipus Rex.

"Are you sure you weren't seen? I thought we arranged I'd phone you in there once Annie had let me know what the ash cash-flow situation was at the Bank of Ash by the River."

Ratatok whipped his paw over his mouth. He'd bitten his tongue on all those sharp ashes.

"Panic, man, panic! You surely don't need to be told the situation – it's dire, man, dire! Do you not get it? Nobody's about – we don't need this stupid secrecy. No wonder you got nowhere! Honestly! The lowest grades ever known to get a diploma – only given to you, no doubt, because some soft otter of an invigilator took pity on your twitchy little tremulous snout drivelling on the exam paper in terror of the questions! Good Odin, Ratatok, you don't think squirrel! You dither like a man and have to wait till Annie tells you the situation. No wonder you're only a lesser-known species of dead-ordinary, third-rate, lousy bird louse, broken-winded bandaging GP!"

"But I wanted to make sure the coast was clear. I didn't want you set upon by brigands when you're carrying such a special cargo and ..."

"And nuts!" cut in the Professor, interrupting Ratatok's whining. "It doesn't matter, then, if I'm vandalised when not carrying special cargo eh? No one's about, idiot – they're at the bank panicking. Of course the coast is clear. A battling stag with one antler up his nose, one in his eye and another up his backside would have been aware of that. He wouldn't need to wait for Annie out of the harem to tell him!"

Dr Ratatok looked hurt. Dr Ratatok was hurt. Professor Oedipus Rex was a past master at hurting Dr Ratatok. Dr Ratatok had always been somewhat scared of him and had often undergone such verbal slaughter as this. The onslaught would go on – it always did. This one had still a bit to run.

"It's that quiet, I was skipping along whistling – as you see, resplendent in my bright-yellow scarf and pink trilby – in full view, and not a soul viewed me. Then I hid in the ruddy wet bush to please you." There was something wild in Oedipus's eyes.

Ratatok, glancing up from the floor he was studying, happened to catch his look in an instant of fleeting view. It wasn't wild anger, it was wild despair – and that shouldn't have been there if what he was supposed to be carrying was, as it was supposed to be, the answer to all their problems. Third rate or not, Dr Ratatok knew wild despair pretends to be wild anger, often to hide its hurt and give its self-blame an object for its self-loathing to kick at. The present object, Dr Ratatok, cunningly decided to poke at the wild-eyed look a little.

"But what you're carrying could be the subject of international intrigue and plots by spies to get hold of," whispered Ratatok, paddling his paws in the air for extra effect and to get Oedipus to keep his squeaks down.

"Maybe I was carting it, but I'm not now." The voice had gone from a big-cheese tyrant to little, meek, baby-squirrel child.

"You've not ..."

"Lost it?" The Professor finished off the enquiry for the Doctor. "Not exactly."

An uncomfortable silence followed, broken – after a brief but seemingly long moment – by the door bursting open and Lochran's ear-piercing loud words were heard on becalmed air.

"Dad, I've come to confess! Oh you've your bosom squirrel chum, the referred Professor Oedipus Rex, with you I'll come back later."

"No, you damn well won't! Any confessing won't wait. I'm in no mood for verbs that'll keep us fed on doing words until supper. Now speak. The revered professor would love to hear."

Was there a teeny note of sarcasm there?

"I've joined the Carbonari, Dad."

Jaws fell open, and the air itself stopped leaning on its elbow, listening to Oedipus with rapt attention, and held its breath to see what came next. Lungs paused the world over and birds fell from the sky. Lochran's jaw remained as limp as usual as he entered the stunned surgery and awaited the world's return.

Meanwhile, Lochran's earwig went off and he told Ransid, his muscular brother and refuse collector, or dust-squirrel, by profession, that it was safe to enter as his father was well aware of the Carbonari matter and hadn't said a word against it, Ransid would be okay to tell him his news, too.

Ransid had been waiting in the busy bush, both brothers having decided that the nut is a softer bite than the bullet, and with all due deference delicacy and tact they had decided to tell their father quietly of their respective involvement with dangerous outlawed terrorist organisations. They had been waiting until there were few patients around, and on this day most of them were hysterical at the riverbank.

An insensitive and potentially public-riot-inducing national-emergency pamphlet had been published by Wood Doings, the national daily paper. The paper had also induced panic with the headline, 'Save Soul and Cash by Raiding the Bank in the Morning. All Hope Gone. We're All Going to Die before Nightfall Tomorrow Evening.' Neither The Doings, as it was known, or its national-emergency pamphlet was free (the publishers wished to make as much cash out of the job as possible).

By spreading the erroneous 'news' that there was only one night left, it was hoped that everyone would think they might as well have a good time and spend their money before they die. The publishers hoped to get rich as they owned much of the wood's businesses, including rowan-berry-punch places, cafes, gyms and red-light areas.

Though Ransid had been given his brother's reassurance, he did not particularly like the sound of bitter recriminations, livid with anger and frustration, threats, accusations and dirty linen being washed in someone's blood, or Lochran's screams of agonising pain emanating from the surgery across the clearing.

He stood and wondered why the air had seemed to clear off, as if the trees daren't move in case they were seen by whatever was causing this noisy scene. Ransid, being a well-built, no nonsense belligerent punk squirrel, didn't go in for knocking knees. His progress towards the closed door – which he did believe actually shook continuously and bulged outwards now and again – was sensible and vigilant, but unimpeded by the terror or horror he felt. As Ransid had often banged punk tree pipits and even bigger punks' heads into barn doors and parked barks, he thought he recognised the source of the sound every time the surgery door and surgery itself bounced. If it was, as Lochran had said, 'safe,' then why wasn't it the sound 'safe' made?

Suddenly the door was flung open and Lochran fell out, flat on his nose, only to disappear inside again in an instant, dragged by the legs at quite remarkable and impressive speed, unconscious, on his stomach.

By now Ransid had arrived. He saw it was Dr Ratatok doing the dragging, as all good fathers should drag their children (even unto the nearest river to drown to put out their misery of money won't suffice and put their misery right) should their kids be flattened by life.

"Why, Dad is that old geezer squirrel sat staring in an upturned chair between its legs at the ceiling? Why is your desk overturned? Why is Lochran dead or having one of his fainty do's? What's Great-Uncle's picture and your medical diploma doing round his neck, Dad?"

"It's all a bit of a mess, son," said his father.

Lochran on the floor stirred, nose twitching a little at the ceiling as he lay on his back, tail upright till it bent like a question mark.

"Your brother has announced that he's a Carbonari, which is okay by me," explained Dr Ratatok. "His hero, Lord Byron, was one when he went freedom fighting – and it's a good cause he's signed up to, carbon's fight for freedom from human abuse. It's just like the Methane Monkeys in the jungle, who claim humans have no right to break wind, they pretend to be above us animals, and so, by rights, have in theory forfeited all rights to do so. "You can act like a fart, but you've lost the art and all you do is be one' is, though, the longest, maybe most inspiring, call to arms ever. Methane as a gas is in a class of its own – and is perfectly okay, and knows its place with animals who act natural. But, left to the backsides of human kind, 'too much of a good thing leads to silent springs,' the Carbonari says. Those same Carbonaris are sick to death of carbon carrying the can for every fossil's decision to deal in some coal- or oil-coloured black market. It's as if carbon were a Mafia boss and fossil leaves and fish its gangsters when, all along, human avarice sees to it that seas are rising and the coal and oil that ought to be sleeping is whipped into serving men and women's greed."

Ransid thought his father knew an awful lot about the wood underground, but he'd never have given his old man credit for it before now.

Lochran observed, "Oh Father, how touchingly sensitive is your beautiful poetic narrative! The analysis is brilliant and I'm sure Lord Byron would have loved you beside him when he died for the cause in Greece. He loved animals, especially big dogs and turkeys."

Dr Ratatok did not like big dogs and had once been chased by a turkey, who he later learned was a brave fellow who gave his life for a Christmas dinner. He's since then had the greatest respect for a breed who lived their lives aware they would die, stoically trying to cut down the amount of methane people expelled. Sadly the species had the mistaken belief that their white meat gave off less gas than red, when passed.

Since then he'd loved and respected all freedom fighters, mistaken in their causes or not. There were tears in Dr Ratatok's eyes at the thought of such courage, tears of love for his father in Ransid's, and tears in Lochran's as he staggered to his feet half in his head and half out.

"My old friend Professor Oedipus Rex over there, gazing as if he's out of it, is out of it. He's flipped, as you punks say."

Punk squirrels don't say it, but Ransid didn't correct his newly exalted father to the ranks of anarchic hero.

"He's – as long as I've known him, right back to university days – had a very, very low tolerance to stress. No sooner had your brother got his Carbonari off his chest than Oedipus had one of his do's and turned violent.

"Violent?" Ransid and Lochran repeated together – only Lochran's was in an attitude of 'that's some understatement' while Ransid's was more in an attitude of shock, awe, wonder and surprise that a gentle, academic, widely admired squirrel could be so – well, violent.

"I know." Ransid nodded emphatically. "You don't have to tell me. He got upset and lost it over Lochran's involvement with an outlawed terrorist organisation. There's a dirty great split along the top of your desk, Dad."

He'd stopped being emphatic and was looking around. Dr Ratatok ignored him. The obvious would need paying out for, not pointing out. Lochran's eyes were still looking in opposite directions, the daze in them aware there were two desks with splits in them – one over there and one not really fixed at all, but circulating, a kind of oblong wooden planet with drawers instead of satellites circulating round it. Oh yes, and there was an old gentleman squirrel circulating while seated on an upturned chair.

It was like a beautiful ballet against a starry sky. The first desk was about to be launched into space by a squirrel with a Mohican. A brave venture, the first rocket sent into space by the squirrel race! The first of the inter-wood squirrel space race! See who gets to far-off Planet Earth first, the grey or the red.

Lochran was still a little out of his head as a result of its repeated contact with the door, so, regarding anything herein repeated as coming from his lips, remember that Lochran was not all himself at the time.

"The old gentleman underneath the chair up there had his earwig go off, and then he went for me," said Lochran.

Here I'll digress again. Earwigs make a lucrative living signing up with Vodawig. Vodawig'll give the insect as much free, unmetered call time on its own nippers as it likes. In exchange, the wig gives to customers who sign up eighteen month contracts with it – access to nip the wig, whenever it tickles or runs about on a flat surface, to an ear to hear who's calling from nippers at the other end. As earwigs are telepathic it's easy for one to get a signal for the purpose of communication.

On the occasion of the Professor's mobile going off, it had chosen the moment (a random thing left to the discretion of employee earwigs) to give him his latest monthly Vodawig bill (purely an unfortunate coincidence) just as Lochran ended his confession about being a Carbonari man. The Professor, under stress and pressure, both personally and in his profession, at the time, simply flipped his wig.

The poet squirrel is a delicate and sensitive creature. A golden soul kind of radiates from him for all to feel, to be aware of, and often even to see. Lochran was a real bad example of this so soft and sensitive that one might say 'limp' – not in a pejorative, sense of being meek or weak, but just 'limp' as in damp or wet, something you'd like to wring out, as his father often wished to do.

This golden limpness got up some creatures' noses and made him a natural target, as it were. However, though the bulging of the door from inside was Lochran's head and backside being continually banged against it, the poet, for one so limp, was extraordinarily thick-skinned. The skin had formed enough scar tissue over the years to make him not just a good poet, but a great one.

"Was it a very bad bill then, Dad?" Ransid, out of genuine concern, asked.

He himself had had big bills, too, from Vodawig and was thinking of terminating his contract once it came up for renewal and persuading his wig to go 'wig as you go' (pay for it as you go along) by offering it a lucrative piece of rotten wood. There'd be no end of rotten wood around, what with ash die-back, and the contract would be cheap to run with no banker's order up front because there'd be no banks except the new, green, flat and pleasant one of an ash-bank-free riverbank where you could sit and chat on your wig all day to mates' miles away.

"Have you been or are you leaving!" Ransid made a hasty return from idle dreaming. His father was bawling sarcastically in his ear. "George, go look at the Professor. He's just slid off his perch on the bottom of the upturned chair and as his bottom sat him on the floor the chair rolled over him, missing his head by a butterfly's width. It is now the right way up, facing him. You can go and pick him up and seat him in it. If you'd been here with us, George, you'd have seen all of it instead of being somewhere off daydreaming."

George was Ransid's first name, actually – the one he'd been 'oaked' (we say christened) with at birth. The name George was only used when he was up before the bench for being drunk and a nuisance, or not drunk but a nuisance, or when his father was mad with him. Ransid, never too old to be scolded by his father, never answered him back or questioned him. Though it was his name, if his mother used 'George' she'd get one of Ransid's dirty punches. Lochran hadn't said 'George' since he was five - he made very sure when speaking of the poet that it was always 'Lord' and never, never George.

If Lochran envied his brother anything, though, it was his first name. He often sighingly thought to himself, "Two brothers in a family, one a great poet, the other a great thug, and the thug has Byron's first name and the poet is named after a Ratatok ancestor who founded a nut-storing firm in a moth-eaten hollow tree, ran off with his foreman's squirrel and ditched her in Scotland before disappearing with a price of ash keys on his head for doing the dirty on her. And gradually whole broods of young squirrels turned up, claiming him as their father and saying they were heirs to his fortune.

They never found Lochran the First, though. He disappeared completely without trace in complete disgrace, though it's doubtful whether he was much bothered. Lochran the Second cheered himself with the thought that Byron would have appreciated the irony. Lord Lochran Byron was much darker and Byronic, given where it came from, than mere George, who was just a king and a hard working farmer, after all.

Ransid didn't like the Professor's colour at all by the time he had made his way through the smashed surgery and got the lolling squirrel into the chair.

"Dad," called George, "I don't like his colour It's the wrong red."

"Well done, son," returned Dr Ratatok.

By this time Ransid had cleared a path and his father and Lochran had got there.

"What's he trying to splutter? See if you can make sense of it while I give him a thorn shot dipped in nothing. In an emergency, when there's nothing to dip it in, the prick itself is good enough to raise the dead and even the Professor, if stuck in with enough professional 'umph.' He's got an erratic heartbeat – an arrhythmia. Presumably it is a heartbeat I feel – unless it's his wallet I can feel beating a hasty retreat before a victorious Vodawig."

"That's good, Dad," Lochran, though still in space, was finding life full of poetry, "A fine line of profound poetry to be lost in the daily battle of our surviving lives!"

"If you say so, Lochran, get a sterilised thorn out of the drawer on the floor there. Brush the dust off it. Use your tail for this. Tails are good as they're never far away and always handy. Yours is perfect right now as the blood on it'll lubricate the thorn and make it easier to go in our thick-skinned colleague here. Spit on it, then. Get some antibodies on it. Then jab it in someplace while Ransid and I hold him down!"

Getting more and more agitated in his rambling, incoherent state whilst Dr Ratatok had been dishing instructions, Oedipus grabbed hold of Dr Ratatok's arm and tried to heave himself out of the chair. As he pulled Ransid and Ratatok down, both struggled manfully to hold him down in the chair. Mad, wild, staring eyes gazed up at Ratatok.

"He looks to me as if he's got Ancient Mariner syndrome," observed Lochran.

"Stop peering over in between him and me. Go get the shot, as I've told you, and shoot him, Lochran," squawked Ratatok, full squeak.

"No, they shot the albatross!" squeaked Professor Oedipus, madly fixing the Doctor with those mad, wild eyes.

"What albatross is that, then?" enquired Ratatok, admirably calm while Ransid and he tried to restrain the Professor, who was heaving like a deeply troubled sea. Ransid's great hairy arms were getting tired easily – surprising in view of the way he could bulge them while showing off. In actuality they weren't too strong.

"Just beach muscles of the kind all young squirrels hanker after," thought Ratatok, anxiously watching him tire and wishing with all his heart his son was the anchor his muscles only suggested and pretended to be.

Suddenly his son turned into the anchor and proved his father wrong – not the first time he'd been wrong about either son.

"Have a rest, Dad. Put into port a mo, as it were, while I hold your daft shipmate down with one arm while inscribing in the air – poetic like – the flight of the albatross he and Lochran are waffling on about. To answer your question, Dad, the albatross in question is the old bird shot by the crew in Samuel Taylor Coal Tit's epic poetic saga The Rhyme of the Ancient Bartender."

Lochran, by now on his way to seek for sterilised thorns in dark corners, thought about querying with his brother the 'Bartender' part, but as his head hurt he couldn't be certain of the facts, Maybe it wasn't 'Mariner' after all.

Ransid continued his English creature-literature lecture, one arm waving theatrically about the other shoving the still heaving Oedipus down in the chair. Dr Ratatok puffed, stood and looked.

"This Ancient Bartender geezer was wiping glasses out at this wedding reception when in staggers this smartly dressed young sea captain with a frown on his brow. "What ho, my

77

mariner mate!' says the pump-puller, who knows this admiral or whatever bloke of old. 'Long time no see. Have you been at sea?' That's a bit of the poetry in there, see. 'See' rhymes with 'sea' – see?"

Lochran and Dr Ratatok nodded together.

"Well," continued Ransid, "such a story the First Sea Lord or whatever tells the bartender. His unruly crew breaks all the rules by shooting an albatross, which is bad luck – and thus they shoot themselves in the foot.

The worst thing a sailor can do is shoot one of these big seagulls cos their ghost doesn't forget and comes back and sees to it that you get becalmed and all that and your teeth drop out because you only get tinned custard because the ghost gulls get all the wind to drop out of your sails and you can't go and fetch bananas from a nice island to go with it."

Ransid stopped to thump the increasingly writhing and agitated professor, who was becoming a distraction to Ransid's discourse. During the short time the Professor was out cold, Dr Ratatok asked Ransid about something he felt wasn't yet clear from his son's eloquent explanation and obviously deep knowledge of English creature romantic literature.

"What exactly is this to do with the Professor Ransid? Why was this bartender ancient?"

"Double shift, Dad – he looked older than he was. He was tired – haggard, if you like. He needed the overtime as he had a big family cos he was a bartender."

"Do bartenders have big families, son?"

"They did in those days, Dad." Ransid, having cleared his father's query for him, continued, but as it was getting late and was part time for his high-protein shake (with added casein), he decided to cut corners to get on. "Lochran – him supposed to be a poet – doesn't know it all by a long way. To hand it to him, though, he's right about Ancient Mariner syndrome and how the Professor's a bad case of it," conceded Ransid. "Wild, mad, starry eyes and incompetent rambling!"

"Incoherent!" called Lochran, unseen but heard over in the dim corner.

"Eh? If you like, that as well," called Ransid. "By the time his young friend the Admiral has finished, the already knackered bartender from all those extra overtime hours is about out on his knees."

"He's got mad, wild, starry eyes, I suppose, just like the Professor – right?" said Dr Ratatok, flat-like.

"Yeah, and he's been drinking a bit to keep awake – a bit too much actually, so he's rambling a bit by the time the young captain carries him home over his shoulder."

"Where did you study this, Ransid?"

Dr Ratatok wasn't the least interested. It's simply the kind of thing one asks when one's stopped caring about anything.

"In bed."

"I thought as much," replied Dr Ratatok, flat-like.

"In bed with chiffchaff pox as a kid, with Lochran sitting beside me – captured audience – reading it."

"Captured, if not captivated," observed the done-caring doctor flatly, without a becalmed breath of emotion.

His two remaining unspoken questions were, "How had the young admiral got back to dry land off a becalmed ship?" and, "What happened to his unruly crew?" Maybe they had only just got out of port when it all happened. Maybe they swam to shore in that case. But that was unlikely because no bananas grow in Lincolnshire (Coal Tit was a Lincolnshire tit) – not even that long ago – and they must have been further away before they became entirely reliant on tinned custard.

These questions had to remain unanswered as the Professor was becoming more rambling and his eyes, mad, wild and staring, bartender-like, were growing larger still as Lochran out of his corner with a thorn ready, shot it into the Professor, only just missing his father by flinches. Ratatok rejoined Ransid to help restrain his increasing chair-bound writhing.

Silence is not golden – golden is noisy. Silence is green – the true silence only the wood experiences at times. You may recall from eons ago that our saga really started with Lochran's confession. Both sons had things to get off their chests to their father.

During the green silence, which lasted but such a brief time after Lochran shot the Professor and he instantly calmed down, Ransid turned to his father and said, "Dad, I've joined the Mickey Mice."

His father replied, flat-like, "Good for you, son."

But the Professor was not at all flat-like – indeed, to reveal exuberant enthusiastic stare, his eyelids shot up and, as if electrified he sat up, fully aware, with such speed that he startled the three squirrels gathering strength together there.

"Indeed, I see Lochran's point thought there's no actual Ancient Mariner syndrome, medically speaking. It's a delirium temporary, like that of the overworked, overtired bartender rat – with a few too many crafty sips on the side. By the time he got home on the captain's back he would be delirious, wild-eyed and seemingly mad, gibbering on to his wife about the captain's adventures. And one throwing himself around – er, and others in bad cases (sorry Lochran), while suffering uncontrollable convulsions – is like a raging sea. And what's more, I'm quite becalmed now, too, as you see.

Beauty is truth and truth beauty – poets always come up with so apt a phrase. It may not be placed in any medical dictionary as a condition's name, but is would help the relatively ignorant wood dweller to comprehend his illness better."

"If," thought Dr Ratatok, "that wood dweller had studied O-level mammalian in English countryside literature!"

The Professor – definitely himself again – characteristically steered his preaching in a nasty, hurtful direction, "Reassuring it is for squirrel-kind that a mind like Lochran's finds its true level at the top of his generation for creativity and artistic expression. His words will be a wise influence on both his peers and no doubt squirreline and general wood intellectualism for centuries to come. It is so godly heart-warming that a child from such an unpromising, ordinary, poor-quality bloodline of mediocre mammals should rise above the dustbin-emptying and dull, common, cold-nose-wiping prescribing surroundings of his birth."

Dr Ratatok noted the steam coming out of Ransid's almost horizontal ears – like the steam from one of those fangled jet fighter planes which kept groaning over the wood from nearby Conningsly The delta-wing configuration matched his son's ears and the steam from the engine outlets matched the steam building up as Ransid was about to scream down on Oedipus.

Ratatok didn't want to witness the attack. He imagined his son ending up in a court of law. Deftly the doctor took the subject off in another direction, "What upset you so, dear friend? Lochran's confession to being a Carbonari – the genius bard you admire so deeply becoming a member of the nasty party – or losing the precious potion you were supposed to bring to show me years ago this morning?"

"No my Vodawig bill" came the reply. "The last straw it was. I'll fill you in on the whole bundle of hay that came before it Your sons may as well know about the priceless preparation that would have saved the world from pernicious ash die-back disease."

It was so long since Ratatok had heard about that that he couldn't place what it was for a moment.

"Your father and I go back a long way and though he never realised his full (or a sip, even) potential, I trust his judgement. I wanted his advice on how we could market this potion to humankind without disclosing out laboratory's whereabouts and how we're so much brighter than them."

"Is 'market' a slip of the whiskers quite innocent, or does it disclose a mercenary intent?" wondered Ratatok.

Oedipus continued, "I've a shield bug – had a shield bug – with enough doctorates to decorate a gymnasium full of the brightest human minds known to mankind all working out at once. Shield bugs as a species, have the loftiest ideals of any creature. That shield is to safeguard all life, to defend and champion all good causes. It is the symbol of bravery itself. A shield bug would die sooner than give up the fight. The shield bug is probably God's greatest achievement."

"Though I never got far, I am aware of that," commented Dr Ratatok, dry flat.

"I work out a bit, Professor," said Ransid brightly, forgetting his detestation of Oedipus for a moment. He was lost in his beloved love of pumping iron off abandoned joy rider transports and junked metal machine parts. "Feel this bicep – and you can thump me on the top of my tail when I straighten and raise it horizontally in your face. I won't flinch even a little. Control, Professor! Control of the body and emotions! You get that through working the carts and pumping springy tree branches while standing on one fairly close beneath."

"Yes, but you all three have one thing in common," observed Dr Ratatok wearily. "You've got muscular mouths developed through pumping wind in the dictionary of life. You Ransid and your brother – with Annie as your superb trainer – you've weighted every sentence with the strength of the same twenty-six letters pumped by humankind and lifted off us in the first place. You'd never huff and puff two or three letters when an absolute queue of them would do. I mean, instead of a lightweight 'Yes,' we might see the tongue lift six heavy words, straining and going down on one knee to get the purchase and thrust to get the tongue to push a 'Yes indeed, that's okay by me.' And instead of 'No' we might see the bulging triceps forked tongue doing 'No, I'm not at all happy about anything surrounding the negative I have to give.' That's fifteen full jaw shifts. No wonder the muscular prowess of your mouths is renowned the woods over!

And as for you, dear old friend at university in your prime you had huge beach muscles developed by puffing your chest out in the gym, and you trained your teeth in rapid cardiovascular repeats of 'I am him you all seek to squeak in adulation of and believe in as the coming of the prophesied squirrel massive of ancient squirreline scripture.' All those mighty heavy words when 'I'm a big-headed sod' would have sufficed!"

Complete silence ensued. It continued for a moment or two Three squirrels then as one, started to clap and stamp.

"Bravo! Ho, what a workout Ratatok!" heartily complimented Professor Oedipus.

Lochran handed his father a towel.

"Odin's horse, you've a memory, sir! How well I recall those heady days. The words I'd heft with my muscular eloquence charmed the ladies of every species I met on campus. They heightened to the full the university experience of maidens from newts to coots and beavers to buzzards

. All were whimpering for more of what my bulging eloquence could lift out of the greatest book ever written You all know the sheer size of Twitchwold the Redlug's venerable encyclopaedic comprehensive treatise on language, the laws and the thesaurus implication of every word in every tongue, vernacular, regional and get-down street-dirty-wise, The Alphabeticus Squirrelineca. It's where the language we speak originated. For that great, great work Twitchwold required the keys of 4,000 ash trees to write it on. That book told the creatures of the wood to, quote, 'Let mankind have it but don't tell him where it came from.' Of course we didn't give him the book literally – it's far too precious to give to heathens. Twitchwold the Redlug was using language heavily – you know, read between the lines, circumscribes and elisions. He meant, in short – or if you like, in its lightweight form – 'Give him a key, but not the tree.' That's why for instance; we only gave English twenty-six letters and not the 326 of the original English alphabet.

The same goes for every other tongue – we gave only enough from Twitchwold's book to get them talking and warring, lying and conniving. We now use only twenty six letters too, to keep us in touch with man's false tongue so that we keep our verbal eyes sharpened, if you like. If we practise constantly his tongue, he can't sneak up on us. We keep abreast of man by keeping our lung muscles as strong – stronger, in fact – than his are."

Dr Ratatok, Lochran and Ransid were stamping, cheering and clapping. It was as if a harmonious brotherhood of like muscular minds had been born behind that small surgery door on the morn of the world's greatest need when threatened with annihilating disease. Ratatok suddenly snapped out of it. Words were a drug and he'd had enough. Depression and the face-aching, jaw-breaking tiredness of heaving too many purple-patch painted heavy words about, hit him like a barbell dropped from the top of a dying ash tree.

"Please tell us where the phial of ash-dieback antidote is, Professor."

Dr Ratatok felt he was getting near to hanging upside down around with his tail hanging down and his whiskers upright in the air, from the same poorly ash tree maybe. With this question solemnity re-entered the surgery.

The Professor was subdued in his reply, "I used the pre-production Phial One to be certain the preparation worked. It was enough for ten sick ash and all ten lived. Phial Two was made overnight, after ear wigging you the news and arranging our meeting for early today. At six this morning I put the warm phial on the open window ledge to cool, made breakfast and sat before the window, eating breakfast and thinking about the priceless stuff in front of me in the little bottle.

My genius shield bug of a lab technician – like all such talented, gifted insects – is a very physically frail individual. If there's one character fault shield bugs have on account of their high-principal way of going about, it's that they don't trust anyone – not even a squirrel with nearly as many degrees as he had. In short, he'd never tell me the formula of his ash-dieback antidote.

He said the two worlds of us and them would learn as one – their UN Treaty Organisation, our own Forest Foundation for Wood Well-Being, their Medicins sans frontiers and our Medicine Sans Bugs, Flowers and Animals. He said that at the right time they'd get either e-cash mails or small bottles left on laboratory tables by the secret-service cockroaches (those in dark glasses so they aren't noticed). It could be analysed to ascertain its composition after they tried it at home on the poorly ash in their garden, as advised on the label left with them. Any road, it didn't go down like that as it happened.

Cyril's health gave out. He had spent long nights without sleep trying to perfect his answer to the tree disease." The Professor swallowed hard, wiped a tear from his whiskers and threw another off his nose.

"We buried him at 5.30, just as the sun was rising. Cyril and I were up all last night preparing the second phial. What courage! Because wigs were as big as him, he got a mate of his to wig his lovely wife, children, aunties and uncles and tell them he was dying and was unlikely to last the night. Even those ash trees that have natural immunity and had helped us so much in our research were said to be weeping as the news spread fast, carried by shield bugs who'd been part of his team. (They were not privy to his formula as they hadn't enough degrees to get a handle on what he was working on they believed it was a medicine for sick ash keys).

Anyway, even his disabled old friend Aunt Marmacete, as he jokingly called her (you'll recall her as a fellow student from college days, Ratatok), and his Uncle John (with the bad cough) were with him 'n' me all night long waiting for him to peg out before dawn broke. (They weren't a nuisance – they just slept or played monopoly in the room next to our lab). Every now and again one would look in to see if he was still with us. When he did finally peg out, it was such a touching funeral, especially as his formula died with him."

All four squirrels were weeping loudly and profusely.

"Didn't you peep over Cyril's shoulder ever – get some idea at least regarding what goes in it?" wailed Dr Ratatok.

"He didn't have shoulders!" wailed Professor Oedipus Rex.

"Shielded it, did he?" wailed Ransid.

"He trusted no one, being so very high-principled!" wailed Lochran "How empty the world will be without such a one as he!" wailed Lochran a wail more.

The Professor dried up. The day was getting on and there had been tears enough. He thought it must have gone lunchtime by now. Oedipus only got where he was by being harder than he looked, though it must be said he looked hard enough, or would have done were it not for the very battered-by-now pink hat – still in place – and the yellow scarf he had been using to wipe his face before handing it round to the others. Each of them twisted it in both paws before passing it on (a subconscious gesture, surely, indicating their attitude towards one standing before them who they'd have loved to strangle).

"I was munching towards breakfast end – the funeral guests having long gone – preparing myself to ignore all your hysterical instructions, Ratatok, about hiding the phial to get it safely to the surgery. I knew in my own mind I wouldn't be stopped or bothered in the least because every wood inhabitant was panicking over his cash ash at the bank.

Suddenly I heard the sound of someone's heavy breathing. Blockhead Brock, on a morning training run, stopped in front of the window, snatched the phial off the ledge, swallowed it in one, ran off and was gone."

Dennis 'Blockhead' Brock was all-Lincolnshire boxing champion. His nickname came from his reputed ability as an infant pup to wake his mother up by head butting her whenever he wanted to thump a sibling, just so that she could watch and cheer. She would be his appreciative audience, as it were. Perhaps it ought to have been her who was so nicknamed as she let him carry on in his bullying ways.

Dennis survived a culling attempt, and the bullet wound was healing nicely in response to Dr Ratatok's treatment, but

Dennis was back at it, running early and sparring in the afternoons, preparing for a comeback fight with a 'white stripe' or south paw. Though nocturnal, those of this species who turn to sport – for they are a surprisingly athletic sort – wear shades with oak-leaf frames and tinted spider's web lenses. (Fragile, expensive oak-leaf tints can only be afforded by the most successful daylight-training, nocturnal-sporty individuals found in all species).

"Well," went on Oedipus, "on the one paw, it's understandable. Blockhead saw a delicious-looking blackberry-coloured liquid and it was reachable through a window. He was parched so he grabbed it and was off on his travels again. On the other paw, it's stealing. Not just that, you'd think it'd taste so bad he'd spit it out."

"On the third paw," butted in Dr Ratatok, "Blockhead didn't get that name just because of his other's favouritism. He's often punch-drunk from nutting his mother and being nutted by contestants – and probably since his childhood, by irate brothers and sister. Once he came to me with an arse full of pellets, and he thought he'd got a reaction to the puddle pudding his mother makes. He says he's got a delicate gut, and he's been harping on about it ever since I prescribed his first bottle of child-strength nightshade antacid when his mother brought him to me years ago, but puddle pudding's not what you'd choose if that were true. I mean, owl pellets soaked in a muddy puddle and cooked on ash mark six for only seven minutes   as is the tradition – are not good for delicate digestions. They are no better than a phial of ash-dieback-brewed Blackberry Bull energy drink, I think."

"That's good stuff I always use," chipped in Ransid brightly. "Rudge Bullocks energy drinks sponsor F1 sycamore racing. It's what we drink at the gym or while watching seeds going hell for leather at a throwing circuit where you get close to their adjustable rear wings. And I wouldn't dream of going on a Mickey Mice anarchy-party march without it. It helps you overturn gundog and farm-cat drink dishes and knock washing-powder packets into kitchen sinks when we go on mischievous larks at the expense of humans."

"I'll squeak with you later about that, Ransid," came the non-wit-had-sunken-in-response from Dr Ratatok.

The serious-minded though controversial Carbonari were one thing the outlawed little-terror terrorist organisation the Mickey Mice, run by a council of brigand field mice, most with extensive criminal records and hell-bent on having a good time at humankind's expense was quite another.

The Carbonari he could empathise with. The black balaclava-clad mice, known for raping rape fields and pillaging bathroom toothpaste by biting the tube so it oozed out when squeezed, were beneath contempt – especially for someone Ransid's size of respectable parentage.

Originally the Mickey Mice had been a small item of news on page three of a bunch of ash keys. Now, since opening membership to all species hot-, cold- or no-blooded, they'd become something of a sizeable nuisance. Dr Ratatok – too tired to prevent digressions by gently closing the digresser's eyes for sleep and wrapping it tail around itself – through force of will stopped himself nodding off on the comfort of Blockhead Badger's digestive problems and Ransid's anarchistic mickey-taking plots. He must focus on the world-threatening elephant in the surgery. He tried to concentrate on Professor Oedipus's long-winded filling-in of space where digressions thrived unless filled with elephant droppings.

"So we've lost the thing that could have saved us all."

The bleakness of the droppings – the smell of their implications – got to the four of them. Three of them took their leave. The mental images of withered ash keys withering on dying trees left with them. Dr Ratatok stood watching them go, all three (sons and old friend) had embraced and kissed.

This day had forged a deep link between four squirrels in the punches and bruises, sharings and carings, upsings and downsings and elephant muck stuck to their shared red fur. A ceremony of despair! Keep your Carbonari and Mickey Mice!

As Ratatok watched his sons and old chum shake paws, about to go their separate ways and disappear into the bush, he had thoughts of a sort of red-fur brotherhood in his mind, dawning and shiny in his black eyes. All three turned as one and looked back at him. Odin's blood, as one they saluted him. Thoughts of the brotherhood shone in their eyes too.

Dr Ratatok sniffed. He closed the door, now extremely creaky on its hinges. He paused, the hinges not bothering him.

"What if this brotherhood, perhaps to be named the Tails of Justice, met together in this surgery whenever a crisis dawned and emergency called? What if four trauma-tossed and friendship-tested brethren met, with Cyril Shield Bug as their sacred emblem – whenever justice and order was threatened? Problems righted and difficulties surmounted, Cyril's fine, proud, handsome features could be left behind them on ash-leaf tokens – a symbol which would come to represent courage, renewed hope and restored justice. Cyril's rallying image could one day appear on the marching banners of people seeking freedom from tyranny the world over.

Whiskers a-twitch with emotion, Dr Ratatok righted his chair and shoved it beside the one his beloved chum had sat in there. Soon he was asleep. The door opened and Annie closed it softly. Her loving smile left to get out of the way in case she looked around. Ratatok stirred, opened an eye and saw his wife glaring down.

"Have you gone through it, beloved?"

Blind to her husband's one or two less admirable sides including his temper and his tendency to jump in the deep end and get his fur wet – she was short-sighted enough never to see as far as any side but his. Those sides were constantly lit in the most radiant light her love and loyalty could shine.

He'd no chance to reply.

"I've just borne witness to a display of the most dreadful and uncouth behaviour, there in the bush."

She deftly up-righted the table, for she was a big squirrel. She seated herself on it, paws folded, facing Ratatok.

"As I came through the bushes, the clearing beautifully lit by the morning ahead of me through the leaves I saw out two sons going one way and Professor Oedipus Rex going the other. It looked to me as if they'd all three just finished a conversation, or a meeting, or something of the kind. I called and the three of them regrouped and came my way. "Have you left Dad, my darlings?" I enquired of our children, to which Ransid, pointing at the Professor, replied, "This stupid geezer has recently lost the answer to the greatest threat ever to face western woods and perhaps the world."

His language was pure Ransid so it's not an exact quote; I've sweetened it a little. I did, however, get the feeling that there is more than a hint of animation in his attitude towards the Professor. You know, I believe it's from my side of the family and in no way are you to blame. Ransid is like my Uncle Joseph, he does nurture the smallest grudge until it's ready to fledge and fly for the throat of the begrudged. Yes, he is so like Joseph."

Annie sighed, shut up and looked down.

Dr Ratatok's shiny black eyes had gone the kind of black they do the insides of pans with. Annie's head suddenly looked up in one quick gesture, her eyes fixing Ratatok's pans to the stove of his slowly simmering fear and apprehension.

"He swore – Ransid! He swore and tore fur out in paw-fulls," she said with all the emphasis sheer awe from recollection could summon.

"His own, I hope," muttered Ratatok cautiously while his own red fur slumped further in the chair.

Annie reassured him, "Oh, yes. Don't worry, dearest. It was Lochran's fur he had a go at, and only after Lochran ran off screaming did he set about the Professor who, giving as good as he got, went for Ransid's ears, trying to tie them in a knot under his chin. No doubt he doesn't want anyone to find out the truth about the so very much admired and venerated Professor Oedipus Res, who I always thought was a horrible little man of a squirrel. I could never stomach him."

"What happened then?" Ratatok had almost disappeared down a rear corner of his red easy chair and he had to repeat the query louder so Annie could catch it.

"I undid him with difficulty, it being a horrid granny knot his ears were tied in. Trying to hold a livid, rampaging, hysterical squirrel off with your tail and the odd backwards kick is not easy while untying your son's ears.

I was wrestling Ransid, too, because he wouldn't be still. He was trying to restrain me all the while from really going for that nasty, nasty squirrel. My son and I left the bush, the howls, squeaks, and cries fading behind us. He was shaking his paws and beating his chest like Tarzan. Ransid and I stayed within the clearing until he'd stopped shaking and the shock and fear had gone from his eyes. You don't expect to be set upon and beaten up by a thug and bully old enough to be your grandsquirrel.

Anyway, I saw Ransid home, settled him in bed with the nice thick blanket we bought him for his birthday and told him to bathe the roots of his ears in his own urine three times daily. The commercial generic stuff from supermarkets and chemists is too weak."

"Too weak for weak knees," muttered Dr Ratatok, though he could have shouted it as there was no fear of being heard so far down was he in the corner of his chair.

The earwig started to run around the table to the side of Annie – as much in joy at having survived the damaged day as for the call someone was making. Annie pounced on it and raised it.

"Hello," she cooed.

Silence while she listened.

"I'm afraid he's backed into something of a corner right now as regards time. There have been so many attempted suicides as well as successful ones, you know, the ash situation being what it is. Everyone's worried to death about making tail ends meet."

Silence while she again listened.

"He's in bed right this moment – ear infection – and will be indisposed for a day or so. I've still to notify the council he'll not be on the carts for a few days."

Dr Ratatok struggled back to the surface of his chair like a red furry submarine with whiskers for periscopes coming to the surface for air.

"Rest assured, Mildew, I will get the Doctor to phone and speak to the lad as soon as he's back from his suicide mission. Promise me you won't let him do anything rash, now. For now, I suggest you get him to rub witch hazel in. As for the other, you say they're beginning to show signs of thriving. Interesting. Tell him just to carry on as he is and – well – continue going there, as it were."

Another silence.

"Yes, indeed – they've been friends since infant school. I will get Ransid to unblock it. Just give him a couple of days. He'll be only too pleased. As is well known, he does a bit of plumbing work on the side."

The read submarine had a vision of one of the Mickey Mice biting into a toothpaste tube. He nervously twitched his periscope. Annie put the wig down. It's hard to tell when a squirrel smiles, face-wise, but you can always tell when they are smiling inside.

"Who?" The submarine wasn't quick enough to avoid the verbal torpedo.

"Mildew Brock. Her lad Dennis – do you remember him, my love? Lovely, angelic and frail little chap! Our Ransid took him under his wing and encouraged him to take up boxing. The rest is history, as they say."

It was mostly mystery to Dr Ratatok – dark mystery. He didn't know where it was going, but he had an awful premonition that it was only going to keep him in the dark till it got to the black hole it was going to deposit him in.

"Well, they want Ransid to unblock their toilet for them. They haven't been able to flush it since about mid-morning when it became blocked. Their fear is there are too many leaves for the rain to flush away."

A sour idea started to curdle in Ratatok's brain, "Blockhead – blocked." Was something coming together?"

"You, Lancy – he wants you to tell him why he's passing bright-green healthy-enough ash keys. They won't flush, you see, so they're having to go in the garden, where they're starting to grow shoots and leaves. This phenomenon, I suppose you'd call it, has only been going on a few hours. He's no idea what's wrong and feels fine apart from the constant vomiting of ash buds and the keys. With the diarrhoea he can hardly get out of the house to the outside lav at the far end of the yard fast enough. Bother! I ought to have told her to make sure he's drinking enough! Dehydration is a fear, as I'm sure you'd be the first to warn, dearest."

Actually, Dr Ratatok would have been the first to say a simple, "Help," He didn't though.

"He was too embarrassed to talk on the phone to me, poor boy, even though I am a doctor's wife. Sweet really," concluded Annie.

Sweet indeed!

This was the last message sent before the full assembled crew of cells saluted on the deck of the brain and the furry submarine dived again.

THE END